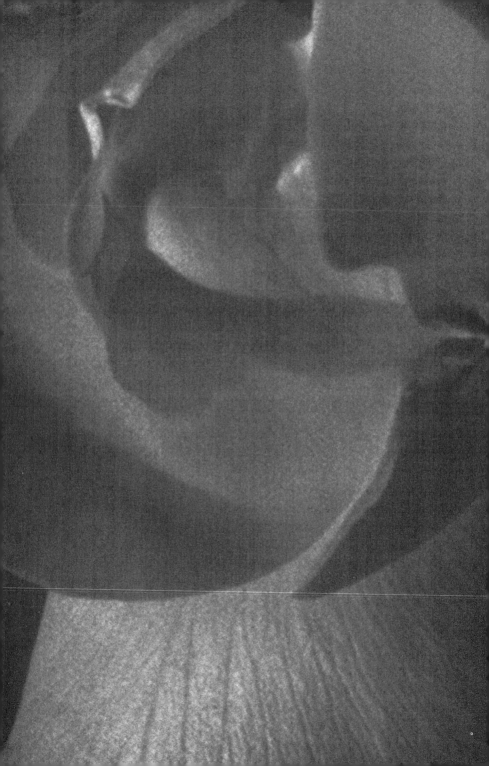

carla harryman

city lights books • san francisco

©1995 by Carla Harryman
All Rights Reserved

10 9 8 7 6 5 4 3 2 1

Cover design by Rex Ray
Book design by Amy Scholder
Typography by Harvest Graphics

Library of Congress Cataloging-in-Publication Data

Harryman, Carla.
    There never was a rose without a thorn / by Carla Harryman
    p.   cm.
    ISBN 0-87286-301-8
    I. Title
    PS3668.A6755T44   1995
    813'.54—dc20   95-9775
                                                             CIP

City Lights Books are available to bookstores through our primary
distributor: Subterranean Company, P.O. Box 160, 265 S. 5th St., Monroe,
OR 97456. 503-847-5274. Toll-free orders 800-274-7826. FAX 503-847-6018.
Our books are also available through library jobbers and regional distributors.
For personal orders and catalogs, please write to City Lights Books,
261 Columbus Avenue, San Francisco, CA 94133.

CITY LIGHTS BOOKS are edited by Lawrence Ferlinghetti and Nancy J. Peters
and published at the City Lights Bookstore, 261 Columbus Avenue, San
Francisco, CA 94133.

ACKNOWLEDGMENTS

Some of the writings have appeared in earlier books including *Memory Play, In the Mode Of, Animal Instincts, Vice, Property,* and *Under the Bridge.*

Acknowledgments are made to the following publications: *Poetics Journal; New American Writing; Zzyzyva; Lingo; Yefief; Mirage; The Columbia Poetry Review; Some Weird Sin.*

"Portraits" and "Speech" are from the manuscript *The Words: After Carl Sandburg's Rootabaga Stories and Jean Paul Sartre.* "Magic (or Rousseau)," "MacArthur," "Margin," "Meghom," "Murdering," "Mud," "Mothering," and "Matter" are from the manuscript *Games.*

"There Never Was A Rose Without A Thorn" was written for a presentation for Nayland Blake's installation *The Philosopher's Suite* at Artspace in San Francisco, 1993.

"Automony Speech" was first presented as a talk at the Detroit Institute of the Arts in 1987.

Works otherwise not cited by Charles Olson, H.D., Socrates, Nigel Dennis, Freud, Raymond Chandler, Dante, Honoré de Balzac, Colette, Michael Taussig, Walter Benjamin, and Saint Augustine appear in fragments in one or more of the following: "Property," "Animal Instincts," "Murdering," "MacArthur (Mimesis)," "The Rock."

The author wishes to acknowledge Sarah Schulman, Robert Glück, and Philip Horvitz for thoughtful readings at various times; Amy Trachtenberg for her on-going participation in the Games; Asa Watten, especially for "The Imitator"; the Wallace Alexander Gerbode Foundation and the Fund for Poetry for support that translates into time; and Amy Scholder, for her intelligent guidance, preference for prose, and commitment to this collection.

for Barrett and play

CONTENTS

PREFACE

THESE HYBRID WRITINGS, STAGED AS THEY ARE BETWEEN FICTION and theory, the domestic and history, abstractions and androgeny, the rational and the nonrational, the creator and her artifact, organize themselves against normative ideas while using whatever tools of novelistic, philosophic, autobiographical, or poetic discourses present themselves to advance their tellings. Concepts such as narrative, character, and binary thinking are manipulated and scrutinized but not adhered to methodically. The writing is also a response to literature and the things of the world: it does not separate one off from the other. Marquis de Sade, rocks, Balzac, war, Lautremont, amazons, Jane Austen, news, Jane Bowles, utopias, Ludwig Wittgenstein, child's play, Saint Augustine, censorship are probable points on its strange map. In the world of this work, words themselves may become characters and instincts are regarded as if they were books. Complex ideas and simple rhetorics mingle, yielding impure theories, precarious stories, and fabulist games.

Carla Harryman

1995

TOY BOATS

I PREFER TO DISTRIBUTE NARRATIVE RATHER THAN DENY IT.

The enemies of narrative are those who believe in it and those who deny it. Both belief and denial throw existence into question. Narrative exists, and arguments either for or against it are false. Narrative is a ping-pong ball among blind spots when considered in the light of its advantages and defects.

Narrative holds within its boundaries both its advantages and defects. It can demonstrate its own development as it mutates throughout history. This is its great advantage. I.e., in accomplishing its mutability, it achieves an ongoing existence.

Narrative might be thought to be a character and its

defects lie in his "potential to observe his own practice of making falsehoods." If this narrative is imitating anything, its intention is to convince the audience to enjoy the imitation, whatever its lack of truth or reasonableness.

Those who object to this artifice are narrative's enemies, but they, too, are part of the story. They are subjects in the hypothetical world of a story. "I" too am a subject of narrative; *I see enemies all around.*

> Because nothing is happening these days, no weather, no fighting, morning and nights, I had thought to begin my account with a little fable or narration. But I have been intercepted en route by a question, attempting to trap in flight that which forms a narration. What does it mean to allow oneself this indulgence? The indulgence of a little story? Meanwhile we have gone down in defeat and my account has entered history.

This is a more or less inaccurate translation of a bit of writing from Jean-Pierre Faye's *Le Récit hunique*. It is a story about the temptation to tell a story whose fate by the mere coincidence of time is to enter history. Faye tells us the story about the story rather than the original story, which has disappeared into history along with the enemy. The original has been replaced with a story that functions as a critique. The critique holds its story up as an example. Or, another way to look at this is that a story can be an example of a story and so serve as a critique.

What Is the Status of Narrative in Your Work?

Oh, the boats are large, are they not?

Whatever gave you that idea?

From looking at myself.

You are introspective?

I am an indication of what occurs around me. For instance, some snakes occur in forests, whereas others occur at the zoo. This is something zoos will not confess, for when you read the labels, snakes occur someplace other than in their cages.

Your argument doesn't follow. You are a bad philosopher.

I am showing you around behind the scenes and you call me a bad philosopher. You don't have to call me anything. Look at those large boats, dream of the ports they have come from. Think of the miscellany they carry, the weapons that can drive anyone into a frenzy of fear and conjure a story. *From out of the blue, the boats descended upon us. We were dwarfed by their size. What were they doing here and why so many? The German and the Mongolian were nearly touching hulls. It was as if they were human and we were ants. The children playing behind us had not yet noticed this ominous display.* But as you can see, I can only make fun of the possibility of your tale.

My tale?

Isn't that what you wanted?

You have no tact, no skills, no frame of, frame of . . .

You mean no plan.

Nor do you produce resemblance or have a serious purpose or struggle with truth.

Or dally in genre literature.

There are no sentiments. It seems we are beginning to find some points of agreement. A resemblance to death and destruction is death and destruction, etc.

Like beans on the same shelf.

Yes, a bond.

The reality principle is continuous with our relationship so we don't have to trace things.

The facts we have come up against are in need of processing.

I don't have to tell a story to make a point.

The story is an example of your point. An ugly howling face comes out of nowhere. It is artfully executed.

You mean a bad boat.

No, you have provided *that* information. But don't get upset by the disparity. A harmonious relationship produces a tedious vanity and a single repetitive conversation . . .

(Then the boat sank, leaving behind them pieces of purple debris floating out of the harbor.)

The question of the status of narrative presupposes a hierarchy of literary values I don't entertain in my work. Narrative is neither an oppressor to be obliterated nor the validating force of all literary impulse.

"You get to the world through the person. Anyway, it's true. And yet, I keep wondering what does this mean in some larger sense? And then I wonder what larger sense I am getting at. There is something on the other side of what I can articulate that grabs the writing to it."

Extension is inside and outside of the writer. But I could also say that the thing pulling the writing toward it is chaos: the words fall in place in anticipation of a jumble. Or equally it could be an as yet unarticulated theory, which if ever made articulate would comprise a number of fragmented histories. Histories that have been intercepted en route by questions. The result might be something like a montage of collapsed ideas. This is a reflection on the enormity of the world. I am not in possession of all the facts.

Because I continue to avoid those absolutes like morning and then night, I can't get back to the original statement. And yet I contradict myself, as these statements distribute themselves in their oblique reference. The word *ground* here comes to mind. The ground is the constructed ideology. Or a world of print.

Do I see the ground but can't make sense of it?

I am already anticipating exhausting this subject.

A structure for writing that comes from anticipation relative to an elsewhere, which to become somewhere—i.e., a writing—must borrow from the things of this world in their partiality.

IN THE MODE OF

IF I COULD IDENTIFY THE USURPERS I WOULD. THERE ARE NO NEW fitting names or titles. All those in use sound antiquarian. What I am referring to is in limbo between history and novelty. Like a story. But the destroyer of the story, instead. Even FBI has a musty, film noir tinge. The steely-brained contemporary law enforcement agent is shadowed by backwardness and low tech. There is little the story will permit me to tell in its present situation. I cry out against its situation. Yo! Since I am not one of the responsible parties.

If. "If the story were snatched away" is a symbolic conjecture. Symbolism is an obstacle to the story's existence. Symbols tend to obviate my own situation as well. As if I were nullified by having been seen eating. As if the appearance of eating stood in for the supreme lie. The creepy setting dries up all but replacement value, one wall after another, or one bite.

Is there a place for me in the obstructed story? I will conclude now that "I" am no more than the story. The "I" identifies with the story in a neutral light. There is no neutral light; therefore, "I" do not know my own sex. Since the story has none of its own. This is not logic but a language of logic used to other ends. Just as "I" might be used, as well, to other ends.

Male and female. Is one thing we generally know about ourselves if only in a blockheaded and parsimonious manner. If female then not male. If male then not female. Each conjecture invests in a separate set of allusions. These allusions evoked by the use of the word male or female are generally identified as behavioral, as set apart from biological, characteristics. I suppose I characterize this manner of naming as parsimonious because of the crimped condition of each term in the conjecture when the allusions invested in each come to maturity.

If. When one says "male" one thinks of a young boy who does not like pony games. If. When one says "female" one thinks of a young girl who does not like killing games. But if. When one says "male" one thinks of a young boy who likes killing games? And when one says "female" one thinks of a young girl who likes pony games? Then it is possible to discuss the use of allusion.

It is startling, don't you think, to be in a crowd and to suddenly notice that you are fully conscious of the sex of each person in the crowd? I have studied female sociality. It shows that females start in the "we've been had" position. Someday, I believe, in the future, this startling knowledge, this inexorable consciousness will create its own self-devouring mechanism. A light will go out. We will see each other first as sets of gestures, postures. And so on in a kind of non–science fiction version of some woman's utopian vision. For right now I contest this gender knowledge and its self-devouring demise by simply not making a claim as to my own gender.

The neutral light seeks an object. It would be impossible to decide the time of conception of the light, the object, or myself; however, this is of little consequence to me as I euphemistically speaking become one with this or that Emile Nolde or Modigliani. My desire to give birth to art has created yet another self-devouring mechanism.

Masturbating in front of the Nolde image is not the most perfect way to confront a Lillithian birthing urge. Nevertheless, I enjoy discovering that the gleam of a flower in this or that painting is identical to my own body's lacquer.

Unfortunately, paintings are about the balance between the animal body and the insensate, and the fully realized eroticization of the painting by the viewer, I have found, destroys the balance. However, my own disconcerting practice has lead me, leads me now, closer to a discovery. It is a discovery I have long planned on "having"; although, the details are not yet and may never be clear.

So here I am standing in front of an expressionist nude, trying to decide how I would view this nude if I were a man and how I would view this nude if I were a woman. If. One is a woman then it is likely she has studied how men look at nudes. If. One is a man has one studied the way a woman looks at nudes? A woman can almost experience a nude in the mode of a man, his fierce desire to disappear into the thing that "wants me most."

I want to tell you that right next to the nude, is a painting of a fully clothed peachy catfaced woman smoking, her smoking arm's elbow not resting on but tipping the back of her chair, her legs crossed flamboyantly, or almost. The painting radiates a redundancy: "I know what I am about." Therefore the adjacent nude continues to claim my attention.

Or grabs it back. It needs it/me. To make something of it/myself. I am wondering. If I were a man. Would this nude make me want to squeeze the cock in the rip of her ass, or to grab under her behind to her pussy? She is, possibly, grotesque, but also possibly completely voluptuous with just some kind of male agony infused into her, so that you can't really see her except through the pain the artist has associated with her. This is why her knees are pinched together, her ass is jutting toward me though also twisting away and her head is turned to look at me with great suspicion, or it is turning away as a gesture of repulsion in what she sees in me, which is what I see in myself if I am a man and want to grab her pussy. Which I do want to do. But am I a man? And is it her pussy? Or mine I would grab first? I'm thinking it over when the collector of the painting stops next to me, greets me, having noticed my "engagement" with the work. I do not know what to say. The collector is situated at an odd angle. Should I respond to the collector while still facing the painting, head-on, like the gawking neophyte that I am, relying on the bleak call of words pushing toward the mouth but then sliding back down the throat just as they touch my lips, as if repulsed by the thought of sex before arousal? After what is probably a painfully long time but possibly only an instant, I realize that I have confused the question about pussy I was asking myself with the greeting from the collector. "I'm only a subsidiary art lover," I say, only in fewer words. In one word, only, I believe and with a look I think the collector will appreciate. Then we each face the painting silently.

Now I try to reawaken those thoughts that compelled the collector to speak to me and that will tie the collector invisibly to me. The collector will want to know more. I say, "If I look at this painting as if I were a woman, it is very different than if I look at it as if I were a man. In the case that I am looking at the painting as if I were a woman, I would say the nude is a man in disguise."

The collector invites me "out to the house" to look at a few more. Suddenly, I have the feeling that I have lost something important or left something out. It is as if I had just watched myself lock my keys in my car. By holding the collector's interest, my attention has wandered away from the object. And yet, it is my attention to the object that has "engaged" the collector's interest. My imagination inflates with a desire for power, while the collector has received an infusion of my imagination. It is a stripped-of-need exchange, and therefore exhilarating even though I am left holding an empty sack and in a semi-pathetic manner look to the collector for something, anything, as he fluffs himself up with the product of my imagination. The collector offers me a large bag of groceries to carry into the house.

The room to which I am escorted is the duplicate of a room in *Notorious*. Is this the discovery? That a fiction is attainable? That one can actually possess the explosive representation of a narrative artifact? That life imitates Hitchcock?

A painting walks into the room supported by the collector. It is the painting of a nude by a contemporary artist.

She is scarred by shadows from venetian blinds. "The ritual scarification of light and shadow," I say. But am thinking, silently, the female nude is the self-ironization of the male. She, in his shadow, by design.

The collector is called away to the phone. I pick up the extension next to the nude and listen to the collector's conversation while stuffing my hand down my clothes and clutching my genitals. The collector is making a large contribution to some fanatics who want to censor art. The removal of nudes from public art spaces will give them the glamour, forbidden pleasure of a black-market item and drive the prices up. I can't tell if this is a preposterous speculation on the part of the collector or inspiration. It seems that the outcome for the collector is terribly unpredictable. What if someone found out?

I want to come before the collector gets off the phone. I look at the nude, her slatted body, her pillarlike knee, the tough looking genital area. But not her face which I choose to avoid as I come into my hand. The collector hangs up and then I do as well, wiping my wet hand on the inside of my clothes. I quickly feel on the bottom of the chair for come that may have seeped through. I realize that I have broken into a light sweat, that my hair is slightly damp, and I smell a little funky.

THE KEY

. . . but I am thinking about Mad Love.[1]

ON THE ISLAND THEY MET AN ARTIST WHO TRAVELED FROM THE
wet side to the dry side each day to work in his gallery. He
was a white man who painted the youngest sister of a deistic
Polynesian triad. Her energies were replicated through the
children he photographed for his paintings, but one time he
painted the deity an ageless woman in profile. Her prominent skull structure, deep eye sockets, and translucent ten-
drils for hair amplifying the artist's horror of maturity.

They were tourists, the woman and child, and the
woman was surprised by his whiteness when the artist
appeared out of the back of the gallery to introduce himself.
Deity though she was, the artist's race made his representation

---

[1] *Mad Love* by André Breton, surrealist meditation on love.

of the Polynesian girl-child shocking. Unexamined puerile desire to dominate gave itself over with free abandon to a spiritual exoticism. The paintings were not prepared to meet an interlocutor face to face, and taking them seriously was a faux pas in any worldly sense, yet the artist's complete commitment to bad interpretation, the devoted care manifest in the work, excited the tourist as if she were between two worlds.

Although she was normally tongue-tied around strangers and cared little about their thoughts, the tourist wanted to quiz this man, whose black-and-white self-portrait hung on the wall: in it he presented himself as a male-female dyad. The painting had the romantic effect of an over-enlarged facsimile of a tinted photograph. The man/woman version of the same face was divided by a power-spear of light that resembled the iconographic mythic pastiche of superhero cards. The negating palate of the painting protected this spiritual-illumination from overt subjectivity, as if the artist had been able to transform his "divine inspiration" into a style of industrial knowledge, something "to be" culturally palatable. Yet, the work naggingly recalled to mind the criticism men, when in need of explanation of something that does not quite fit, level on women: they are too subjective. Regardless of the present context, it irritated her that she couldn't get this thought out of her head, it being such a poor substitute for pleasure.

The tourist considered how to approach her examination. What questions were the right questions? She looked at the man, who seemed as happy and somber as any aging man in paradise, and was reminded of L.

She had met L in a seedy Parisian hotel in the vicinity of the Pantheon nearly a quarter of a century ago. L was in love with a sixteen-year-old, Isabelle, who came in her school uniform and string of pearls most afternoons to visit him in his collapsing den. The tourist, who was then herself a very young woman, was curious enough to make herself a nuisance at these transgressive afternoon rendezvous. She lusted after the older L too, but her sociological curiosity got the better of her and she relinquished her competing desires in order to investigate the mystique of the French teenager. The young American sputtered, spoke in bad French, ignored the hints to leave and did everything she could to get Isabelle alone so that she could size up her charm. She failed completely. The younger woman would never leave the presence of L even for a minute, even when he was sunk in a broken chair in a drunken stupor.

Years later, a lover told the tourist in masculine triumph, you don't understand pussy. She tried to ridicule his sense of possessiveness, but later, secretly, she agreed. If the word pussy was reinvested with her own desires—or did she mean reinvested with curiosity—it would have nothing to do with what was typically meant. Therefore, when she used the word herself, which she did as much as possible, men ran from her as if she were a medieval leper.

Back in the "present," she was trying to find some mindful way of asking the gallery artists if any of the paintings had anything, consciously, to do with the history of those Polynesian people whose cosmos was entirely sexual, but she wanted to avoid focusing this man's attention on her own sexual being, which even an academic question about sex would risk. In any case, her young son was standing at her side scrutinizing the paintings himself, and she did not want to disturb his pleasures. "You were being gross," he would have said as authoritatively as the surrealist André Breton.

THE SEX STORY

SOME NUDE WOMEN DANCE TOGETHER.

I've got to see more country weighing on me, stinking long-distance time spans. Floating night, flash-in-the-pan turns into suspicious movie. The screen lights up and the fig flickers through.

Eyes make wide for me. I don't really think too much, but look hard—from stretches in the attic getting voluptuous in one of those light triangles. The sun pours in. Mere potholes enticingly fill with streets others have come to tread, but I am upstairs. Neat.

Monumental monuments of men say wake up. I agree. You have to, just staring. It hurts. That's why it's good to follow couples with your eyes and not move. It's sad not to be big.

This woman has a white apron and they are holding hands down a street I've never been on before. Cornstalks melting in the mouths of reapers, grain elevators churning with ruptured seed . . . I've been trying to get the sex story but it's hard not to be crowded out. You have to watch them doggedly going down the road between monoliths to get the impact. The woman stands in the center of the big ribbon, the road line, and he wraps her up so she's relaxed. He's all around her the way she wants, that's what I hope.

The daylight is coming in for thrills. Grimy facades seared to corners. Naked, tied, and down on my knees in a forlorn beseeching prayer position, I promise chicken Lancelot of Morose Algae Stagnant Lake, in time, I will never tell a joke again that doesn't hurt somebody. Spill-over into anonymous shoe passing.

The lady is not a lady but a pupil in the center of a rim for a prototype carriage spinning its wheels in the display case in the museum, parading for little boys. The lone couple make it on the ribbon, splayed-out, while an approaching cement mixer churns in front of the camera and the giant equipment sheds and storage bins hold little speckled pieces of grit. It's so hot the couple can't get run over. The sluggish machines are too late. She's had hers.

The little boys poke at each other by the elephants. I wish I could weep with delight or rub myself against the tusks. Someone whispers in my ear, "To be always present is a thing of the past," just like mating a hurricane.

VICE

You're just so I don't know all over the place he
was saying to me in his fin position which he
deliberately held until I noticed him holding it
with the breaking eggs in my hand and trying to
get them into a jar before I had to give up. I mean
this is life and you have such a strange approach,
he said. I told him I didn't notice. That's the
point, he said. He was squishing dimes between
the thumb and index finger of his left hand
because he needed to make use of his hand.

The mountains were larger and darker than any I had ever
imagined and no one was surprised but me. When I men-

tioned my surprise, I felt that I was shrinking in their eyes. It
was a little like confessing I'd never had a sex fantasy and in
the meantime we were still approaching the very black pass

> Small velvety hands I could eat out of if I could
> get close to them before the critical moment and
> the dime bends like a bottle top, the useful mak-
> ing the useful useless, I say not expecting any-
> thing in response except the next subject possibly
> too large of approach. Another species would be
> easier to seduce I am about to say before he takes
> me in, shelter from the storm and all those kind
> of dance steps. What a show-off I say and don't
> can't take that back because

we were about to ascend in a car no warmer and probably
not much more efficient than an ox-cart. I looked around to
see who was wearing gloves and counted three men and two
women but forgot the gloves because I started thinking
about what each of us might have for a career and when I
got to my own career I thought about who I would like to
seduce and how would my career fit with that person's so for
instance the professional dancers might prefer a business
executive to a policewoman but a zoologist would be even
better and so I thought if I prefer the dancer I will become
a zoologist but dancers are so physical they're not sexual,
not physically vulnerable and usually emotionally immature
I was thinking because at that moment I was on the verge of
becoming an underground cartoonist and who ever heard
of drawing something perfectly beautiful in that case so I
thought I would work on the ex-trucker now engineer not as

a waitress or a schoolteacher but as a lighthouse keeper but
he was driving

> It's humiliating to say, "oh, that's just from my sub-
> conscious." I bet you make mistakes like that too,
> only probably not as often. And then he says, yes
> but I usually turn it into a joke or at least use it as
> some kind of flirtation. But one doesn't always
> have to be on time I say, handing him more dimes
> as if courting boredom is better than going home
> defeated. I'll just sit here and figure out what he's
> going to do next with those delicious hands and
> then after I can't stand to look at them any longer
> I'll leave my card with the embossed interlocked
> couple beneath a tilted world with no address or
> phone number just an idea

so it's going to be nothing. I mean I'm going to be nothing
because that's more interesting than anything and if I decide
to go after the historian next to the window looking out the
window I will pretend to be a clothes designer pretending
he's a manufacturer of clothes and he won't be able to tell if
I'm serious or not if I really think he's someone who only
looks like someone else until he either shrugs me off and
stays an historian or gives in and becomes nothing too, and the
trick then will be not to tell him not to be honest and senti-
mental but continue to change colors names motifs just to
see what happens when the car gets to where it is we're
going. In this dark eye of the storm we can be optimistic, we
can be good, because we can only see each other, though
there seems to be fewer of us than I thought I had noted but

that's because of these fantastic leaves brushing against the windows with drops the size of thumbnails running down them glistening secretly in the black mess we are inching our way through with some purpose I'd be willing to take back

If you just apply some pressure and concentrate you can do anything you want, it's so obvious, he says. And I look at him hungrily, you mean I'll succeed, I say. And he says yes but you're artless and have you ever heard of artless pressure or concentration. Of course not, I say. For just a minute I had actually not noticed what he looked like. Suddenly I had the very peculiar sensation that I was going back to a time when I didn't know anything when people were opaque and their physical presences overbearing as a consequence and I was looking at him while a splashy invitation to leave overtly looped his torso. My audacity was blotched by overuse. The objet d'art and the artist are the same thing is what I thought but didn't say a thing except come with me to a dance which ended up being a front for a female cult in the center of a modern-day labyrinth housed in a postmodern office building, the outer area of which was an enormous ballroom. So we were to take our position as foils for

MATTER

LOVE WAS ALONE WITH LOVE. AND THERE WAS NOTHING I COULD do about it. Love was alone with love. Why make another move? Why move? It's your turn over there, someone said, and I thought I'm going to open my legs and see what happens. Hurry up, lay down your cards. The cards were in my hand. I put down the card to see what would happen while I opened my legs. You open now, I said. And love responded quickly. You are a good player. Have you been playing long? I learned from an expert, said love. Is the expert still living. Yes, she is. A she, I said. Love was impatient and wanted to know if I had another move. I closed my legs up to see if that counted. Look at your hand, said love trying to be patient. And you, I said, prefer these cards over other forms of excitement. If you can't play, you'll never meet the expert, love replied. I didn't really care, but my body was standing on end at the thought of fucking. When I saw that I and my body were not the same, I knew what card to play and played it as soon as my turn came without second-guessing my opponent's position in the game.

IN THE DOME OF THE IMITATOR

WRITING CUTS OUT SHADOWS. DOMESTIC LANGUAGE IS RHYTHMIC. These are stories.[1] The crack of gunshot outside results in no picture: nothing from the window through which light pleats the telephone wires and patches of gardens and dead grass. There is no one with a hand clutched to a gunshot wound in the arm parodying a movie or a person dead or alive, lying half on the sidewalk, half in the street, elbows and hips dipped in the gutter water, or even a group of people surrounding a victim. Who knows? Weeds grow out of the juniper. The Jerusalem sage's floppy leaves swell, as soft as hair coating an arm. Writing over what was written over is promise of a further heat in place of extra words. The father, drawing with his son, takes lessons from the son on composing superheroes with ovals, arranged in a line down the length of the paper, as guides. The father draws "The Performer." The son draws "The Imitator." The Imitator is so powerful one can't map his power. The phone rings and is not answered in this inside that gets fought for, without being named, against an outside structuring that sometimes gets translated as a name. All this is accompanied by several ifs that are forgotten while the phrase "a variety of" drifts into a remote landscape lacking the structure of skepticism that writing claims as reducible only to itself or that more gunshots crack. Accompanied by screaming and shrieks as if an enormous crowd is implicated. Again the window is consulted and what is there are children skating in free abandon up and down an apartment driveway. "If they don't come in they'll be in trouble," rants somebody over their wild sounds. A dying down of shrieks and the bass of "Can't Touch This" presents a backdrop for the adolescent passing on foot to offer the peace sign to the window from which the music seems most closely associated and for the neighbor across the street in the upper-most corner apartment working out on an Exercycle, her child gripping the balcony railing bobbing back and forth to the rhythm of his mother's panting. The phone rings and is answered. All parties are fine, "with civilization coming to an end," jokes the caller who has recently been reading a news magazine. It is strange to be fine as if one were in an earthquake where the neighbor's house has been demolished and in one's own house only one plate is smashed. The friends agree to meet at the museum on Friday. The child returns with his Imitator complete, the face he claims being the only thing that can imitate itself, but it is also the only thing that can't imitate anything but itself. Something is understood that is so complex that the understanding can't grasp the concept of imitation all at once. The child gets milk and cookies and ice cream and more milk. Voices come from next door, and as they fade, unabsorbable bird chatter blankets this small universe with its noise. Out the window, in the bedroom, moonlight slips through the branches of a brittle pine and the muscular arms of the oak. In bed, the man and woman wonder about the mockingbird in unison and discuss when it will start up, fearing its starting up in the night, usually a little after midnight and sometimes going on until five or so. Not only do they not have their own songs but they take over other's nests and do violence to their victim's eggs. They are nasty predators but their singing and shrieking can be as entertaining as a fine oration, compelling, playing on one's wish for an orator, a leader, and to be taken over by something outside. The child persuades the mother to sleep with him for a little while and when he is out, finally, the mother wakens and slips out of his bed, the squirrels now having joined the mockingbird, whose voice has secured an echo somehow, providing an illusion that there are two mockingbirds when there is only one rising into discussion with the squirrel while repeating each of the squirrels' noise sequences.

The man is skeptical when the woman tells him that *Playback* is Chandler's last novel. He says, "I thought it was *The Long Goodbye.*" He picks up the book and reads the back cover, turns the page to a passage describing cars like carcasses piled against a freeway barrier. He laughs. A child's voice from over a fence addresses a barking dog over a voice in the phone machine recording next door. The woman attempts to explain Lyotard's idea of domus to the man sitting under the live oak on a bench, his pencil now posed to his work. "It sounds very exalted." Domus is only a memory that still holds civilization together. Exalted nonsense holds the family together and the Imitator: with the womblike triangulations softened into shapes resembling boulders hanging down below the center of the Imitator's body on either side of which apish hands grip weapons, a scythe and something less pointedly weaponlike. "If he were cut out he would be three-dimensional," the child explains. "As a drawing he has only two dimensions." A squirrel is spotted climbing the live oak with a piece of cheesecloth that had been left on a bottle in which once had resided ten large crickets kept to feed to the gecko living in a terrarium indoors. The ants have eaten the crickets before they are fed to the gecko and the jar left outside with the cheesecloth still covering it. The superstition is that if one brings the jar inside, the ants will somehow sense to follow it there. Is it possible that ants can colonize the gecko's terrarium and sting it to death as they have done to the crickets? Ants eat the aphids on the Rose of Sharon. They are now in the bathroom and seem to be attracted to the orchid; although, that may be just a fantasy, or a memory of some other, flesh-devouring plant doing battle with ants over prey. The squirrel runs up the plumcot and leaps onto the oak. A white paper sack hangs from one of the oak's branches and it is thought, with great excitement, that the squirrel will deposit the cloth into the sack but he passes it and moves higher up and out of sight. It is then noticed that a plastic sack is hanging from the branch of the pine tree and with some concern the ground is scanned for other plastic.

The mockingbird stops singing at 6:14 A.M. by the bedroom clock. All night long its song, so-called, cut into the quiet without abolishing the quiet but calling attention to it as if scissoring almost laconically across a piece of paper. Or another way to think about it and thinking about it does recur with or without the attention given to it in writing, especially when wakened by it, is that the quiet of the night is a giant cage containing the mockingbird's song. Sometimes the imagination strains to see through the cage trying to isolate the living being contained in the cage. But if the caged being is a song, it is the ear that "sees" and forces out of the way the pragmatic context in which people presumably sleep. Last night, the mockingbird whistled three times as if communicating with a partner over a fence. Strange reports hurtle back and forth disguised as routines; thus at 9:00 A.M. the mockingbird picked up where it had left off before dawn. Since 9:30 three planes have flown over the houses. The passing of the planes recalls the horizon of sound over which one can not hear. The mockingbird announces the obliteration of the horizon. The phone rings. The man who answers says, "so the market is just dead," speaking facts with the benign equanimity of one who accepts facts. Accepted are the mockingbird and the death of the market. And if not accepted? But no one proposed the mockingbird as part of the real estate of the neighborhood. One is relieved from thinking about the pluses and the minuses of the neighborhood when the market is dead.

The mockingbird is the ideal fluffed up in the Hollywood of Birdland. The crip in the crimp detailed and polished so the hair shines brashly. Or two southern democrats running as first ladies for president since suits are going out of fashion.

On the car radio someone is narrating a story live in a warm old-geezer voice. The story is about a man who in somewhere like Skinkville USA owns a tavern and doesn't want to die giving change for a candy bar, so he is contemplating selling his tavern and going on the road in an RV with his wife. His last moments of nighttime sentience drift in and out of their own poignancy as his ideal universe unfolds, smog-laden in traffic with people making contact through the windows of their cars. It is easier for people to flirt when they are surrounded by metal and traveling at high speeds than when they are sitting in cafes is what he thinks. In a chic cafe a young man tells a young woman that only special people should be parents. "My parents were not special enough." In his room the child explains to his friend that artists have the most power next to the president. "They were the ones who helped make the copyright symbol." The man tells the woman as they stand in the kitchen with coffee that he wishes she hadn't brought up *To Kill a Mockingbird,* because now he is tempted to kill the mockingbird. But where is the mockingbird? She has never seen it, and how would one kill it without a gun? She tells him she had thought about shooting it herself but that the thought disgusted her. He says, "No, it isn't like you." In Balzac, if one has a job, one is the job and visa versa. A detective a detective, a prostitute a prostitute, a criminal a criminal, a matron a matron, painters are painters. As if existence were a profession. People build foundations on what they are and if they are double, their foundations are unstable. In Balzac, only poets are split. And so the killer of a particular species of bird would be continuous with the identity, which would be continuous with fate. Marlowe comes closer to this pre-existential neoplatonic 19th century European ideal than most American characters with their typical histories of bad choices, which create remainders, those things one might have been; although, Lyotard would characterize "remainder" as inert, not something left in charge of "the human." The writing tests the concept outside the theorist's bearings, since it takes an alienated view of transcendence. Here a job is not something one is but like a place to live, something one has or does not have. Even the doctor is not the doctor in the nostalgic realm of platonic ideals but someone whose house burned down in the hill fire while taking a pulse. A woman and a girl walk homelessly to the corner church for lunch, and like faux heroines with guns in Marlowe's universe, they do "not raise their voices even a semitone." In time, Marlowe himself has become less a type than a prototype, marking the beginning of a series of repeated gestures turning men into boys who charmingly twist language. What will happen next? The mockingbird has been spotted and it is smaller than one would think, flying tipping this way and that. The yelps it derives from the neighborhood stock noise accompanies any form of attention: the girl's inside the woman, the boy's inside the man. But what of the child? Completely a child, he appears to assume the mockingbird as part of a stable environment in which there seems to be no separation between a thought and a sound.

[1.] From François Lyotard's "Domus," collected in *The Inhuman*.

SPEECH

GESTURES ARE IMPOSSIBLE TO DESCRIBE. ALTHOUGH SIMILE IS over-used, people shudder when anyone pronounces the word femininity. Although metaphor is over-used, description flees to the hinterlands. Everything glistens under the clouds. Femininity can't be narrated. A theory develops that only what can be ignored can be narrated. Cactus, can it be ignored? And femininity is all. Present, never left to be ignored, it is a subject of aggravation. Cactus needles stuck to everybodys' bodies. And the sticky sweet but sustaining fruit. Actor zombies coming out of the arsenals in flames in film memorialize the word femininity. Although metonymy is over-used, no one notices its femininity. This is the same as saying everybody notices it all the time but won't talk.

Sometimes someone looks up at the staggering sky with its willowing undulations and asks, "What are the soldiers to do?" But metonymy is recalcitrant. She urges herself sidewise flushing the question with a limpid wind. Ignorance solidifies a sky that can not be ignored in honor of simile. The structure for narration, because of the culture's abhorrence of femininity. This is not a picture of a culture. The culture having been emasculated. Ignorance begins to be equated with choice: the metaphor not to perceive, the metonymy not to know, the epistle. Eventually less is perceived, less is known less returns to the structures of narration. Femininity never changes but continues emasculation. Everything, masculinity, is memorialized. Everywhere men, women, children live inside penises. After the monument has replaced narrative altogether a cloud called femininity

darkens the streets. Drinking up even Sylvia and so searing gradually dwells permanently in the house of the over-used metaphor: omission. The only thing not feminized are the monuments, the metaphor metonymies of presimilitude. The ity, the first ity, before itty bitty and historicity and narrativity was femininity. She married incongruity. We should never have permitted this marriage. It was the isolation of those two elements: femininity and incongruity that preserved masculine culture. Of course, we don't really know this any more because our consciousness has been emasculated. Now all of the terrain, natural and not, doorknobs, ground cover and dumps, anything step by step grounded and grinding, graded. All in some sequence of gradualness, the endlessly lateral present material which the lyric poem exploded, shaped into monuments but could not isolate.

AUTONOMY SPEECH[1]

Autonomy never wins. *No objects, spaces, or boundaries are sacred in themselves.*[2]

Ideas have autonomy. *But illegitimate offspring are often unfaithful to their origins.*

Picture someone in an entirely autonomous space. *Their fathers after all are inessential.*

This is the basis for understanding heterogeneity released without a form.

Is that uninterrupted thought?

What happens when they have to pee?

The thought has been interrupted by the realm of the corruptible. But couldn't corruption have its own autonomy of purpose?

Corruption is like a cloned idea. But it only works through interaction.

Through instructions blinded animals adhere to peaceful transformations. We are all within reach of starlight.

When I close my eyes I think of a psychological autonomy: there is someone in the room who makes all her own distinctions, who does not use others' covert instructions as a basis for response: this is character: the human form liberated from a trellis of human forms but still surrounded by bathtub, plates, and a bowl of artichokes.

When I close my eyes I am in a room of psychological space. Behind me a lawyer **sanguine** argues a case without pleading, without humiliating the designated criminal. By arguing in this manner she destroys the system of the court. She loses the case and yet weeds out the truth. You can't cling to her statements or twist them. They can neither be expanded nor reduced. When a synopsis of the trial is produced, her part is the only part quoted in its totality because if reduced, it doesn't exist. Her speeches remind the writer of sentences, loose bombs fulfilling their independent missions, that have gone to heaven, their reward for being exactly what they set out to be.

"I don't talk to everyone but everyone I talk to is horrified by these arrests."

The homeless are in the park protesting the ten o'clock curfew. After four nights of arresting people, the police refuse to participate. The City of Berkeley will not press charges because it doesn't want the cases taken to court. It won't give up control, but finally the people, through their unified efforts, prevail in their demand to "be tried."

Autonomy is an idea. I want to move autonomously through a microscopic kingdom of wild urges.

What's outside (scary monster in driving rain) looks inward (a clean biotic stomach infused with natural light). Traditionally, the art museum has been viewed as a "tranquil showcase for art." Scholars, historians, and critics have used this image throughout its history as a means of thinking about the art museum's inherent values and by them it has been compared to **dick** such vastly different structures as temples and churches, libraries, warehouses, and mausoleums and has thus been perceived as a site of worship, contemplation, and scholastic research, as a vast storage container and morgue for useless objects. Depicted in no place, yet surrounded by constituents, a Velcro bib simulating a roulette wheel under his chin, Duarte, for example, rises from his saddle to extend his greetings to the autonomists. Needless to say, my mother taught me to know the value of a neutral subject as well as to relish history. There is little today as salutary as discovering—once again—the sweat of those once-building fools still lingering on top of their ancient creations.

Their fathers after all are inessential.

NANCY: I'm sure she didn't mean exactly that.

DIANE: But I was entirely persuaded that fathers aren't at all necessary. I suppose it is foolish to be dependent on what anybody says, but I am not happy to think of the persuasive speech, which glows in the mind during its delivery, in its aftermath, as just dying embers.

While at work, I think about their debate, and this distraction marginalizes the tremendous implications of my art practice, which is surviving somewhere outside the tropes of work and meaning like a gleeful shepherd on vacation by a lake.

Dick talks about tremendous implications as a means of demonstrating enthusiasm and to let others know they better jump on board before the ship leaves.   **lamb**
Embarked on a lecture by Terry Eagleton on the subject of ideology and aesthetics in the Maude Fife Room among a sea of heads, I become distracted—disturbed by an arithmetical memory: volumes of vocabulary set to verse; and, like the binding, the poems are not revelations within, but rather containers of, books. Inside are quirks—not words—and the sublime— strategies for cell block–type scenarios called germs. Mine is a bourgeois aestheticism for the reason that it purports a universal value and yet it is just a personal feeling. That sentence is showcased in a museum. Am I making *what* I think an object of study? All this stupid wall material (educational blurbs next to paintings) has no negative effect because no one reads it.

GLACIS
In Los Angeles

Then, assay.

Picture lamb in an entirely autonomous space. I find that the athletic reenactment of daily formalities, sick neurotic repetitions of habit essential to survival, create the new. Structure makes it   **straight**
possible for sensory influence to be transformed into communicative acts. The train station, the Japanese

movie, the Irish legend, marches, spiderwebs . . .[3]

But I don't have time for daydreaming anymore. These are the productive years.

Is that uninterrupted thought?

Our art is:

A trap. Nerves under horses' feet. Dust glides in front of a sordid underground lecture. The sky palpitates to our projections. "I will react," we said, and made a man spinning around an eye. The eye is the only feature of our "landscape reserved from biographical writings"—a terrain that miraculously came (Kathy Acker would say "orgasmed") from the pen of Journoud sometime prior to our trip to Milwaukee. What we find **microscope** now is his figure preparing the road. An eclectic is trying to obfuscate our invention: Journoud? Acker? Orgasmed? The road? He will never be able to discern the invention, to weed it out from the borrowed drek. Because we are Cassandra Persephone Pandora A. Propp.[4]

The thinker has been interrupted by the realm of the incorruptible.

"Let me," says Asa.

Pour pepper onto the clay.

Faye,[5] in his story, calls story an indulgence. Why indulgence? asks Thoreau.

Illegitimate offspring are often unfaithful to their origins.

I might have said it is as if lust, glance, sense, fulminating affluent, fulgent, dull fresh dunce, and in such lunch gulch had clustered into a single, coherent and full **crack** sensation. A word can disfigure what is otherwise representative.

There is no autonomy save

the daily

the banal emptied out, the forms of human practices that have no formal language. If there were a formal language for pouring pepper onto the clay no one would ask what happens when you have to pee.

That proposition is from a morgue for useless objects where value is extracted from   **demonstration**

"someone starving in the '50s."

Some things can't be saved.

But couldn't corruption have its own autonomy of purpose?

I want to be mean and loved for my nasty character. Carole A. in her grandiose house in Washington, D.C., lounges with a cigar in her mouth. Abe Fortas talks. It was not in the service of entertainment that the revolutionaries preserved the Louvre from destruction, but she entertains and goes to the office every day. When I get home, I put on her slit-to-the-thighs dress.   **blue**

The boundary between human and animal is thoroughly bleached.

A spiderweb of yarn woven across a Parisian courtyard blocks passage. Nobody will get sick inside shadowless consciousness. Picture the beach. A museum. Some mansions. Each with arms and a grip take hold of boxes. As in fictions, the vast container—a woman in a suburban yard—tingles everywhere.

People of the future will think better while on the move. A child will dress himself in clothes from his father's dirty laundry. Seven pairs of jockey shorts and two T-shirts are now grouped on his three-foot frame. He says he's a circus clown. The parade ends when he needs his "tickle fixed." When the disruptive present meets the evenness of familiar needs

> Dryness and passion
> Don't mix

says the professor. It is best to take her out of the desert, put a few pounds on her and give out bullets of lust. We raise our hand since we   **beg**
realize we've been captured. "Will these words suit, professor?"

> Peach juice
> Slut
> Triple

I can only tell you dryness is not sexy. I would know, I'm a man.

This can't be the University of Milwaukee.

The professor admits that it could not.[6]

Now that we are   **little**
not where we were headed, a tremendous interference weaves into our web of sex.

I asked in a University Museum whether there was a catalogue. I was told that there was not and that there never had been a perfect match. I then went to the University Library and asked the head of the library, who showed me his up-to-date card system. The library did not contain a single volume relating to museums. A printed catalogue nevertheless exists.

It's like a cloned idea that can only exist through interaction.

I don't want to go into that big house. When I close my eyes I'm in a psychological space: people **unearth** moving in and out of rooms performing functions. No objects, spaces, or boundaries are sacred in themselves. According to Vygotsky,[7] inner speech is social. What does that mean?

---

[1] Autonomy speech was written as a talk challenging the notion of autonomy. Its disruptive interleaving of "prior" texts is a mimetic device used to dramatize its premise.

[2] Text in italics is from Donna Harraway's *Cyborg Manifesto.*

[3] A list of influences from a promotional brochure written for Rova Saxophone Quartet.

[4] A trap . . . Propp: transported from the *Wide Road,* a collaboration in manuscript by Carla Harryman and Lyn Hejinian.

[5] See "Toy Boats," page 3.

[6] Dryness and passion . . . The professor admits that it could not, from the *Wide Road.*

[7] *Thought and Language* by L.S. Vygotsky, a Russian psychologist of the early 20th century.

FISH SPEECH

IN THE BEGINNING, THERE WAS NOTHING. NO CATTAILS, NO WIGS,
no paws. There was no doom. No lavender or shirt sleeves.
No burn no yellow or rest. Neither was there beginning. No
light went out. No one held her own against an army of mis-
shapen events. There were no chains. There was no writing
or speech. There was nothing to shave, nothing to swim, and
nothing to cut. Clouds were not clouds. Silence was neither
dominant nor peaceful nor silent. There was no salt or
smell. No twisted seaweed. Or any buoyant flowering possibility of an ambiguous growth. There were no killers and
fleeting lives. There were neither chains of events nor
metaphor. There were no stories or bones. No mulch or
cocoons. No lizard, pelicans, or fish.

In the beginning, there were no instructions and nothing was abstract. There was nothing to identify. And no revision or modification of the description of the thing identified. Neither were there eyes nor touch. There were no millipedes. Earthworms did not nurture the soil. There was no nurturing, no soil, no worms of any kind. There was no inferno.

Sound, word, rhythm, pucker, loss, organization, and signature were nothing. There was no distance. There were no tornadoes and no change in the atmosphere. There was no atmosphere and no alteration. There was no heat, or hint of the future, no possibility of Dante. For hints, futures, possibilities did not exist. There was no extinction.

There were no keys or clues. There was no DNA. Nothing squeezed. There was no singularity or multiplicity. There was no red.

In the beginning, there was nothing to hold and nothing to hold in mind, since there was no beginning, no nothing, and no mind. The end also did not exist. Nothing stopped. There was no gender, no extremes, no image or lack of image and no money. There were no pencils. In the beginning, there were no names.

In the beginning, there was no apoliticized moment of the absolute and no political critiques. Neither was there the hibiscus flowering bearded orchid cunt juices or a male suspect. Neither black nor brown nor white. No maiming and nothing to maim. No future and nothing to preserve.

ARCHITECTURE AND LANDSCAPE
OF ALL COUNTRIES

SOMETIMES IT SEEMS THAT PEOPLE ARE CHILDREN LIVING IN CAVES. The most awesome as well as appealing to live in are those with ice stuck to the walls and tops. The ice droops down so that in places one needs to bend under it. There is so much ice that the fire does not melt the cave, and a child can be comfortable here, wrap herself up by the fire, in blankets, and wait for the next snowfall. When our family moved into the cave, we had to create positions for each member. Mom guarded the cave hole. She sat on the sled. She brought her bandana so her ears wouldn't get cold. Dad carried wood in from the outside. We were afraid his back might become permanently bent under the loads he carried, but he straightened out once the wood had been broken into our fire pot. My brother, who had fallen through ice, shivered by the fire and danced up and down on his soggy shoes. When I got bored I tied and untied my ice skates. Sometimes Mom would play a trumpet from her position at the mouth of the cave, her sheet music propped up on the edge of the sled. If any of us tried to discover what key she played in, she would stick the horn's nozzle right in front of the sheet music so that no one could see the key signature. She kept the flutes and other horns lined up beside her. She said we could use any of them we wanted, which was terrific, except we could never discover the key she played in and for us the notes came out thin in the cold. So most of the time we just listened or warmed the instruments at the fire. We handed them to Mom who exchanged what she had in her hands for the one freshly heated. Most of the time she just played the trumpet, and we were grateful, it was the loudest and least eerie of the instruments.

M U D

WILL IT BE PIG IN THE MUD? BUFFALO IN THE MUD? BABE IN THE mud? Mud pie? Will it be muddy after we go for a walk? Will the game be a walk? Will we be talking to each other? Will we pray to the deity of anarchy? Will the deity pray back, since there is nothing either above or below? Will the mud form creatures known as humans? Will the creatures known as humans make creatures from the mud? Did you know that women have been born from cabbages? I think they have also been born from skyscrapers but what would be really great is to observe the splendid human creatures born from men's suits, lined up in rows, rack after rack. And even with all this variety will the creatures known as humans continue to reproduce from mud? The mud of their own muddy bodies?

Or the aged mud from the ground? That stripped naked and frozen mud that claims to be immortal in spite of our arguments to the contrary and malevolent lust-driven attacks? Will mud in the future mean anything other than mud? Will the amazonian mud woman bring her latest invention to the big city? Will the big city suck all the mud out of her and leave her clean as a freshly whittled stick, scented and vulnerable as the gardenia? Will she demand her mud back? If this were a board game would it be better than Monopoly? Would it be able to compete in the marketplace of games?

My token is the mud woman's invention. Someone else takes the clean stick token. What is yours? Still available is the gardenia, the whittling knife, a piece of money, and a mud patty symbolizing the mud woman's original condition, which we can't quite picture, really, but are asked to illustrate whenever we land on square N(Y)ET: that is in Russian no and in English a trap when spelled NET. After you make an illustration (with one of those stubby pencils with a $1/18$" lead and no eraser) you can advance again as long as no one is two squares in front of you. If a token is two squares in front of you, stop for elbow room: otherwise the mud woman might kill you, destroy your advantage, or covertly lead you to defeat.

MOTHERING (ENIGMA)

"IT'S STILL HERE. IT'S STILL HERE-ER. BE READY. BE READY."
Silently the woman opened. "Oh, look at that. This card says,
there is no opposition left." The door also opened and an
enigmatic male figure walked in. The mother knew how to
be safe and protect her young because of a game she
learned in a song. First she closed the book. There was no
time for pictures, now, and the words went like this:

> Be ready when ready is over the hillside.
> Who, when the light goes out.
> Who, when the light goes out.
> Country the life in a dream.
> City what's left over.

Be ready when ready is over the hillside.

As she sang, she took the hand of the singular man as if he were a little one and led him into a room with a bed. Then she tucked him in, and when he was snoring she grabbed her children, who had by then been sufficiently warned, and fled.

TYPICAL DOMAINS

Z

I ENJOY BEING SLAVISH FOR IN THIS WAY I CONCEAL MY DEEP SUSPI-
cions. I enjoy all the roles I play. When the mayor hands me
a dollop of praise I heckle. I turn on people when they compromise themselves in front of me. My reason is that I am a
hermaphrodite. That is, my reason acts hermaphroditically. I
am normal physically. My mind tells me otherwise, so I nurture my ties with sexuality for slowly evolving transformations.
Nonetheless, it is my intellectual hermaphroditism that signi-
fies, that distinguishes me from others of my background,
placing me in the rank and file of . . . I said I enjoy my position. For what could be the alternative? Do you think I would
be capable of being curt without emulating a big cheese?

Today the satirical mode victimizes me. Picture a cow with a disproportionately large face, horns, and full udder pulled along by her impish offspring. Turn the beast into a human and the offspring vanishes but the effect is the same. As I fumble along I fling pennies into a ditch with a lackey caricature imitating a wealthy kook loved by all. She believes in this love because she can anticipate the needs of her imaginary audience. They are not imaginary in the normal sense but they lack the only ingredient in reality. She is their larger-than-life twin in the comedy. I enjoy playing her role. It has much in common with the secretary, but the boss never appears and the secretary takes over all the duties. Obviousness poses among her accoutrements and supplies her with her hermaphroditic characteristics, well masked.

Concealment is what I most enjoy: I love organs. I have a strong instinct for survival. Speak duality, I say. This is a joke among friends. As I began my address I became absorbed in a question about motivation. Why standardize hermaphroditism with its exotic flavor, its predisposition to preemptive preening speech? Did I want someone to like me or fear me? I think I wanted both. I am by nature reckless, as part of the heap.

Someone else would say get mad. The predisposition to reciprocate bonds identities. The figure standing in front of the boss takes over. She believes in what she's saying. You see that blank in the row of tents? She believes in justice and the eyes of the world. She fends for herself with all eyes upon her. She is a great actress.

I too am a great actress, though I do not savor this part. But I enjoy the part of a man. This is the secret of my charm.

I am opposed to monuments and do not want to be harmed by using language in a straightforward manner; therefore, when I am outside I do not look up.

Everything I have said so far is obvious. When I am reading words, it is never words per se that interest me; nor do suggestiveness, pornography, or universality interest me. However, in that it is about giving one's body up to the unknown, be that a letch or saint or hungry child, I believe pornography suffers from a validity it does not intend. This might be considered a projection or fantasy of an idyllic world, scrub brushes in hand, tiled showers waiting for the naked bodies to appear. They have strewn their brushes in the background but we can see they're there.

Of course I think about sex a lot more than I should.

One evening I put one foot in the clear water. A fish rose to the surface and said, "Euphoria never lasts." I put my second foot in the water and a frog rose to the surface and ate the fish. I swooned and Bill caught me. I was at once relieved of my opinions.

There are no houses east of the bridge.

And then falling.

Boys.

A conservative make.

Somebody says to me, though I can't see why anybody would talk to me since my eyes are deaf to eternity; "You're asking for big trouble, you want someone to control your life." This is Hugh speaking to me from his desk in the lamplight, a diffuse light surrounding the room with munificent flies holding down the files that would otherwise be flipping over in the breeze. He is part of a family one must not omit. He also says, "Imperfection is the motivation for human action." This is a way of spreading generosity as well as accepting a less-than-perfect life.

Today he extracts a cage from a cage and builds wages with belief. Whose? Not mine. This bureaucrat has invited me in to discuss his philosophy because *I have not yet been called.* He can see my imperfections are close to being perfections. But I might grow extra hair and genitalia and get sent to the boiler room where I would be ordered to atone for my monstrosity to the end of my days. In order to avoid this, I have left outside my love of cataclysm—this being the source of the stasis in the office, which Hugh insists I confess to bringing about—so that I might be released from the bondage I have come to love, as a sailor loves helmets.

What clarity? What happy pulse? In this room that is neither inside nor outside? The anteater tongue is held out the window in order to ingest the smells of home. The gravel from the parking lot is occupied by nests of spiders in the corner of the room. Smell of body odor, pine, or lye.

Natural form robs detail of tranquillity.

A pantomime exhausts the nervous town.

Judgment's out the window braking.

A setting followed by taboo.

"I don't know you from Adam but I want you to stay in my shop." This is the summary of a long drama. The entire town becomes involved. Is he a boy or a girl? Is she a man or a woman? Is he the father of her child?

This led them miraculously, perhaps not so miraculously but pleasurably since it was a compromise between the difficult figures formed in the imagination and acts in the world, to release description from objects described so that resemblance to order was denied.

A

On a cool night Z is alone with her work. A basketball player on a Honda stops at her trellis. "Hello, Z, wanna dance?" Z says, "What do you mean?" "Oh, you know, Z." Z writes that down, then places it on a table in front of her and appears to study. Z is always testing people. An endlessly zoolike compulsive childishness flattens out her ironic sleep.

Fern arrives. She says tell Z good night. Fern is like all the people in Virginia Woolf's books—except when she idolizes me. She is always the subject of someone's thought. (Ill from guilt and guilty from illness, she saluted the taxi out of habit, then climbed to M's studio. Her heavy steps signaled the conclusion he had been dreading. His father was right. This gave him some relief. He let her in. As she was removing her hat, he was thinking about the capsized boat and didn't notice her trembling hand. Because, like any of his patients, she was making an effort to act indifferent, he was able to assume the role expected of him.) I have a few more things to say about Fran before we circle back to Z. Fran could adapt to anything, but this never made her happy. She dreamed she survived World War III on a number of occasions and to her this meant nothing. She would not objectify her imagination.

The reason Fern suffers from this sad destitution is she has an analysis of her own experience that doesn't correspond to proven theories. Since she has made herself her own subject (in her own kingdom!), she doesn't believe in professionals. Furthermore she refuses to admit to suffering, because, she says, "I don't experience pain. Pain and pleasure should be taken out of our vocabulary and we should look at our sensations anew." Of course I am loath to condemn her, but it's clearly my job: I know what pain is, as you can see, and so I suggest you find her guilty of subjectivity. The judge rises and everybody drops dead.

"Oh, good," says Baby, "now the air is cleared. Nothing but natural and external causes will interfere with my pleasure again. Furthermore we will all be able to perceive immediately from whence the pain comes." She looks around. "Where do we go from here? Wait. I don't believe in that question. There is nothing of value in the unknown."

In the meantime Z has requested to see Fern. Baby is not willing to inform Z of Fern's demise. Baby doesn't want Z to know how happy she is because Z doesn't believe in happiness. This gives Z the upper hand in all their negotiations. Baby sits down in a red chair and tries to remember their last dispute. "You're scaring me." "No, I'm urging you on." The simplicity of the argument gives Baby a great deal of pleasure. She thinks about how Z would be annoyed with this "memory" since Z thinks something happens then goes away. Then something else happens, then that goes away. At this point Z is nearly hypnotized by all that has come and gone. She looks up and the basketball player is still there waiting for her to dance. Baby is also waiting but can't take the stress, because there'll be a beast.

Everybody wants to like the beast. Traffic fades. The planet circles the Sun. With the details shut out, there is no mystery to focus on. This can be observed in yet another picture. All the people are running around the house looking for the denials Daddy has lost while Daddy has dropped, accidentally, out of the picture.

22

On the beach slaves pass by solving problems.

"This is mere bliss. There must be a better procedure."

"Oh, stop it D, you're tickling me." Beautiful limbs flap in the wind like tortoises out of their shells. Boats run to the beach and slaves pour into them.

The beautiful limbs flapping in the wind said, "D, I don't believe in you."

At this point the creatures projected their identities into climax.

The shadows they cast in battle standardized myth. Correspondence sends speeches to limbo by default. There is upon entering the yellow sea, the blue sea.

"Whose mother are you?" a name asked pulling down her pants.

"Part of the rescue squad," responded the demon pulling at her mustache with her bottom teeth. And then took a scooper and scooped sand, peeled potatoes, etc. She stuffed contradictions into gulls. A mental bank prefigured the divine objet d'art. In the meantime, the creatures who had reached the bottom of the sea had sent their babies to the clouds on ladders made out of the entrails of the demon's progeny.

"Fuck this revolt," said one of the babies. "I am part of that crowd." And she jumped off the ladder into the circus.

This goes on. There are times when everybody wants to lick a machine. The baby wanted to turn the machine off. Now everybody laughs at her in the center of the circus where a two-headed squid mothers her fondly.

The other babies are getting mad because there are too many people in the world. They declaim, "We are not going to work for history, history is going to work for us." When the parents, all lined up at the meat counter, heard this, they started crying and flailing, and the babies untied their parents' shoes which dropped from their feet like children dropping off to sleep in car seats. The babies stepped into the shoes.

Piracy is the first stage of commerce. The babies stand on cubes tearing down houses and throwing the rubble into the train yard in Bellflower. Not far away the yellow sea. Behind that baboons float in the blue sea. The babies have returned us to an illusion of safety. A silence in the shape of a thousand men forms on the horizon.

On the beach slaves pass by solving problems. Surely one can remark on the ellipsis of fate forever! The demon euphemizes the driven things.

"Oh, stop it, D, you're tickling me." Some beautiful imps flip through seeds like torches clinging to shells. The things spit at the imps but the imps can't feel spit.

101

"And this is only half of it," says the troll biting and fingering the water in the road. "The world caves in, the cup is full, the night is long, the day is wide, the field is simple, time sticks out, space bends, hand me some money, dig into your pocket, find me a shave, this is too small, that's better, use your brains, forget what I said, now take off, thank you."

ME: Forget it.

IT: No. On one side the Herculean task. Life flowers

for the busybody in the enlarged fairytale. (Monster = swell milieu.) A peon sees a footprint belonging to the Industrial Brain, a.k.a. the Captain of the Id Train.

Bloated with inherent ideas, the deadhead drives to the store. A figure without parents. And the only one.

ME: Never a whole story.

IT: Right. Happiness and conflict are bound together in such a specimen as we have here. Her sand was the color of his sand, but he was blind.

Again the sun sets behind dogs burying hats. In these shadows the thinking man's son is his undercover mother. She figures in all his preconceptions. Or splits their orbit. Anyway the two of us are filthy. My friends are rushing to me. The unhappy man is less dangerous than the happy man. For this we can thank business.

Fiction acts out the world in which people fit exactly the dimension of one's invention. The feelings are mutual.

Distortion in personality attracts allies because I don't want to. This little secret I keep from my predecessors whose interchangeable parts have the part *they* when I obey. The standard face acts recognized.

ME: That fuses identity to everything.

IT: This is the standard reproach. I hold back the desire to be named. Each night, wearing a different disguise, *she* finks on a guest, then slips back to bed and into her lover's arms. In her lovemaking, I surface with masks that reproduce the tattletale actress. This lousy part promotes me to ace. Now I manage the office on my own but not a day goes by in which I experience an overpowering desire for supervision.

(The theater is all lies. No action represents a human situation. The joke is on the wrong person, and the person behaves as if being hurt is funny. The hermaphrodite flops around in the water instead of courting the ugly queen. The peon places herself at the Industrialist's feet in the Grand Canyon. Someone calls the Industrialist Agnes while he's watching the plague through the back of his head. He is punished for responding to the name. The black forest groans from the strain of his vengeful moans, but the *compañeros* are living it up in their quarters at curfew and don't take this as a bad omen. Next day, everybody wakes up refreshed but alert to the possibility of reversal. Nobody is free of others' responses to them. There is no private space.)

AA

There are times means I was not there, or I will not admit to having been there. In this case I was not there. Not resting in the crook of the squid's bony arm or nuzzled with her hooded nose while the background ministered the other impediments to sleep. There was no decor. So does it concern me at all? Here I pause to think about mammals. I have insisted on one continual stream of statement but have floated away. I have floated the sensibility of the voice or style of the one I am paid to represent at meetings. Imitation is mostly mockery. Cat = 20 + A. But when I assert the authority of the one I am representing, I undermine nothing, and when I assert my own authority, the words are leading me by virtue of the use I have made of them to their surroundings.

While nonmonogamous animals look for mates, work flows out under pressure.

Now to erase the sex from the book I am polishing.

Continuity is perceived by the person who will fill the slot I project my labors onto. In the office I am my function or everybody loses faith. I like this. Everything is work! Now I see someone I know, and my sense of duty mars her beauty, which looks mannered in light of all the "material" I have no ambition to absorb, having become renowned for snap judgments. This was the time when function was mythologized and fate represented in its helpless state.

A machine without operators.

"He knows well how to find himself in a state of complete institutionality."

A dictum here tests the power of gossip by holding it back for twenty years. When the law is violated, the magistrate, whose words are noted to change instantly into our ideas no matter what the banality, says, "Paint the post white," we have erected a monument to Johnson. Then the libidinous newcomer goes and sits on the fence!

PROPERTY

for Barrett Watten

*The rowboat was caught in the mudflats. A few gulls padded
around it. The mud fizzled. A grey mist was broken by a narrow sky.
In the distance a solitary cathedral interfered with the sensuality of
endlessness. The earth was small and even cozy until, looking up at
the beaming monstrosity, one recognized the meagerness of its claim
on space.*

Property

"Come you are a made revolutionary," said her uncle with a
smile. He pointed at the wildflowers. "My vision of the
aspects I more or less fortunately rendered *was*, exactly, my
knowledge. Anything nature puts in the sea comes up. A
fierce man's rainbow is in his head. If there is no Spain? If

there is no Oakland? The original field, once cultivated, returns to high weeds where privacy is absolute. The shape of the story ought to be that of a spiral of doubt. The landscape demolishes the house in our heads. The conclusion is a point of departure for the speculator, but the spectacle is lacking in furniture. The pack of lies is insulted. The song is sung but where do we get the words compelling us to repeat it? My blood runs cold at the sight of death so I tell the story. If the wide obtuse inside is a yardstick in this sanctuary, perhaps the universe views the world like I see a two-dollar bill abandoned in a cashbox. Kiss my ass." He stood up straight.

"Anything pleasurably tolerable but only endurable when it is remembered in the middle of the night, fields we walk on as carelessly as bamboo shoots creaking in the tropics flooded with gross species of rodents nibbling stains on trikes, dictate to any happy man what he can't live without." He held her up so she could be closer. The crystal ball glowed with murk. She cut her finger on the left front fender while trying to smash some limestone with a stick. Her uncle led her back over the property.

Possession
Inside, the ear spins beautiful webs.

"With one clear picture of an individual, collective abstraction is exposed. There is no smoke rising from over there.

"Let me tell you," he swallowed her and spit her out, "it is a bargain."

"Sing to me," she slipped.

"I don't intend," he said, "to imitate poetry but to be imitated by it.

"I live in a fabrication near something I have never said before. I can't see my doctor and when he . . . I do see him he pelts me syntactically. My assignation burns toward abstraction. Because imperatives never blow over, get on your feet! Stumbling through this padded interstice, my body has limits. Yours doesn't compare notes.

"But let me tell you a story. I am civilized:

"The high illusion constrains the pent-up trees. We float beneath them tortoises bathing in the night. It is primitive. We creak in the fog. The outboard motor racket mutes the wall like a powwow. A small echo fishes with a person's features. Me talking fuses to you. Puberty here, fantasy there." He paused, basing his head trip on the profile of a sated barbarian. Then proceeded to deliver his child with unconscious mirth.

Surprised by his use of words, the moral presence swelled to veracity plunging the social salad into the contemporary fork. She looked deep into the merchandiser's past. "Yes," she said, "but you enjoy suffering."

Because there was nothing else, he waded across the pool, fading into a mental fog, which, to this day, fuels its maws with the purest minds.

A robot adjusted her sea in the ornate theater. If this were merely an eidetic image why did she want to be nursed? Nothing stuck out.

It was hot, beautiful. True and the same at the same time. The scooped-out center of the continent described the middle of life without describing a figure. Standing around in serialized plateaus was enough to make one cry. But fleeting mammals sucked up revolt.

Oversensitivity was wrong. She wrenched her mind

from its wasteland of souvenirs. "Where is that bastard?" She couldn't get enough.

He was behind the door, hiding from the spirit of the new world.

Privacy

The insects hung in the air, frozen invisible pouches, contorted parodies of medieval fate. How right for such an afternoon! Do not pull down those varicose blinds. Motion and noise are one thing. The red dragonfly behind the dangling rope is alone forever but the grey has a hundred mates. Brushing aside the air with the power of propagation they yield, like boulders at a hydroelectric plant in Siberia, to the touch obscurity bestows on them via a cook displaying a mound of fried food for two thousand fund-raisers, whose charitable ideas drool, green-eyed, onto the turnstile of insect life so often compared to the web of human saturation points in an adept squirming of an old, an approximately plowed field. A dog's obedience can't be more touching. Everything is allowed to pile up. And why not? Why is the shade thick? The house is lumpy with numbness, protruding from below. And so the quiet day is heavy from a body in a sink.

Expression concludes existence. Though though and though. A thousand red spiders living in brick and that's what refusing to talk is like. Below is below and in is in and this is in. People are surprised. They wake up to find the room, a tiny machine. This is not the time for subjectivity. But it survives. Because space is small. For example, love me but don't talk to me. A size crosses the street. The street asks, what's going on? Some facts are to be gotten around while others remain external to their shapes.

People in the kitchen picking at bones don't want to pay attention to the heavy air. We let them go on—they're not hurting anybody. This special mode of address is used to captivate inanimate objects in our sanctuary. We look at our things because they have our respect.

The Master Mind
"Eve will bruise his head."

The enigma froze behind the triangulated bellow.

"Let me take over."

On another wall, an allegory. Holding her curly head, Cupid touches tongues with Venus. One of her nipples is caught between his fingers which are stretched over her breast. Venus is both sitting up and swooning back, an apple in her left hand down at her side. Her right hand is raised and pointing back behind her, to the confusion back behind her, and away from Cupid's deliciously prominent ass. So in the background of this perfected lust a near-infant cupid is stepping over a dragon about to hurl flowers upon this passion. Some anonymous being is holding rocks. A young girl's head floats on the blue background which a winged god and goddess are holding up. But from behind appears a naked, tortured hag. Cupid is nearly stepping on a dove.

"One thing I always recognize is panic. Such fragility can not go unnoticed to the devils with silks. Are the drainpipes of the bathroom supposed to 'suck' us into the work, and the mock bed to 'envelop' us in its embrace? I stand outside order and look in on its premises. Or take a background of precise historical settings. A romantic bleeds in the foreground while death carts the rest of the picture away. We look on helplessly like children eating candy. Then shove the loads off our backs and obtain permits. And all this in order to understand the external influences that pressed the theme into a particular mold!"

Doors in back streets burst sullenly open.

The guard turns on the underling at the end of the shift. "You are awwk-waard, you are awwk-waard."

The population dispersed when the thunderous voice snapped.

A strange thing, when you come to think of it, this love of Greek, she thought pilfering her uncle's rhetoric. For in the tropics there isn't even a ditch to huddle in. Nor a hole in the landing strip sizing up industrial designs.

Standing behind the door, listening in triumph, uncle noticed the sky. "One forgets to run it down it is so obvious. Daylight without day. Meditate, mediate, what is the difference?" He looked at the same clouds, bent in revery. Concluding that what he heard was good enough but what he thought was even better. But in the back of his mind he was throwing out a rope, he was robbing museums and cracking into tiny parts. He could not blame the other countries.

Acting

The earth is as narrow as the sky is full: a postulation, on a rudimentary level. Clouds protrude to the point of abandoning context. Ducks fly across teasing the edges of clouds with their wings. Reason tells us not to make anything out of these events. Birds fall into the sea. The sea swells, pushing the land under. A seeming eternity, by force. So all that's left is a narrative concealing an error. Contentment is sediment below this image. Passivity has been accomplished through the descriptive process, a mechanism that devours objects, subjecting them to the decay of inner life. Perfection is a disease. Each rock, each sentence suppresses an embryo, elevated as they are to the status of isolated objects to be regarded unto themselves.

There is nothing in the room to look at, unless there is an image to head. In other words, there is no sun in chaos. A vague enigma turns on a deathbed, "Body, body?" The privilege to confuse, the privilege to refuse (canny familiarity with detachable pieces in an unforeseen design: for example, a pseudonym), privileged stupefaction, dazzling, to eat one's words. "You think when I said what I didn't mean I didn't mean it?" A face comes out of hiding the minute one looks the other way, a landscape of inner jargon deprived of the distinction between abstract and concrete.

Derision is the investor in big moves. "When I was born, giants walked the earth." Moving forward, inside the picture, are pieces of a plan. Whether or not it is possible to equally objectify the minutiae of bodily activity and whether or not there is any kind of analogy to be made from personal observation of these discrete exposures, is beyond the realms of *that language* to know. To be well informed is a *matter* requiring a cruder sensibility, i.e., not self-scrutiny.

"I have destroyed my ammunition in order to make myself distinct." To look for an accomplished fact is a word on the other side of a bulldozed tunnel. "Later we'll have dinner, eggs." There is no order to the search. "And I know what I mean eating love." As equipment, something has failed. "This, the creature of habit, brings to the synthetic mind a dead space, or as they say, a moment of relief." She breathed into a glass tube, "The periods of parturition dissolve into moisture." But the frog wants to hold her, to rest his belly on her clavicle and wrap his arms around her neck, to feel the vibrations from her tongue dancing against the walls of his miscellaneous trophy.

The state is drenched in wind and heat.

"Looking up at the sky, I am startled and then eat dirt—opening scene. Anything is possible. In the meantime I have found a bug in the dirt that I devour. The shack crumbles and a few feathers float into the cloudless sky.

"Next scene I am on a cot in a tepee pretending to be a wizened old woman. But look up! Get out of the way. Nibble at a purification ritual and succumb! Shot of dead spiders dangling from webs with maniacal young toady stomping on a lariat while brandishing weapons. Not what you would expect to find at the dump where they're breaking up cars. So get off that rock—the mental picture of one's story and the taste for a particular life. All the juice is in a ditch.

"This is a flower." She cracks eggs into butter.

"Lush, yes. It may well be the grave which is the place for narration. My children are stunted and want the world to be a better place than it is now. There is nothing but perfection in their speech. Let us get to the point of the feminine imagination: 'Suffice it just here that I find the mental bearing I can project the latent historic clue toward—the beast still functions in my hand; again with easy recall I no longer want to marry anyone, but I still dream that I am marrying a very large cat to make a story about art'—Henry James and Colette. Unpaid-for pagans. When I get out of bed a pterodactyl blots out the rattle of my machine."

The path of destruction gouged out its eyes. They sprinkled it with nuts to absorb the pus and walked to town where they were to see a number of weddings. "Auntie, why won't I ever get married?"

"Ask your uncle."

"He's dead, but I'm not, I don't know, and don't even believe you have to die. So what am I talking about? Furthermore, why should I even open my mouth?"

"Your uncle is about to give a speech."

The uncle was standing in the middle of an amphitheater in his bathing suit. "I want everyone in the audience to hold up a . . ."

"Let's come back when he gets hot. I think we are missing something."

"What do you mean?"

"When one thing is entirely different from another, it cannot be in any respect capable of behaving like the other, can it?" Aunt Mildred inserted a powerful fingernail under the corner of the veneer.

"Auntie, auntie, this child is not formed yet."

A Cadillac escorting a bride and groom crossed the intersection. A woman emerged from the dime store with stocks inside a plastic egg. The lights in New York went out. Men came out of the sewers with clubs.

"Hold me, hold me."

All things are now true by inverse. The ocean is heavy below the suspended belly.

SCENE I

Some "deep image" like a three-way collision that occurs beneath the exterior form and as a consequence has no effect on daily habits.

PAM: Sing to me. Let me tell, tell you about, about my education—some likenesses have changed to something else, quasi . . . bird . . . to the point. Am I capable of enjoying a stability of verbal forms? No! I am not capable of understanding because I am a mouth.

> Mirror mirror on the wall
> Who's the mouthpiece for us all?

MIRROR: Noise.

TYKES: (*Just emerged from a pit*)
> Gleeful   Needful
> Gleeful   Needful
> Gleeful   Needful
> Hump!
> Gleeful   Needful
> Gleeful   Needful
> Gleeful   Needful
> Lump!

(They jump into a boat and row out to sea.)

SCENE II

Jungle gym working out with proffered structures. Time: about the time of the discovery of the meaning of their names.

MAY: So, breaking up ground.

HELEN: When one says lily pad but means grasshopper what trick is that? The lily pad sits placidly on stagnant water. We don't get off our asses because there are too many life forms but because the harshness of reality can be eliminated by comparing one thing to another.

PAM: Working for a living and living are the same thing.

MAY: Murder!

SCENE III
Devices of leisure arrive someplace.

MAY: The dregs of society eat me alive.

SCENE IV
Ideas fall into a pit because the sun is always shining on their stomachs.

SCENE V
A collision creates a wrapping around of hostile forms.

MAY: What do you think of a psychology that equates boredom with nothingness? Pretty dumb, huh?

PAM: *(Talking offstage)*
No, I can't *see* they are polar opposites!

SCENE VI
Forced to wear clothes, consults an image.

MOTHER: *(In a tree)* Horace Mann? Now who is Horace Mann? Go look it up.

MOTHER: Now I want you to bring me the pietà.

CHILD: All gone!

MAY: Sitting on a fence post watching all the feet go by.

HELEN: Easy come, easy go.
(Throws a big chili pepper at May)

The child fled into a jar and turned the dials.

". . . supplying intensity and chronic confusion to imprints on the lacquered tiles. My report of experience is my appreciation of it: pinning down this equation to the ensemble of animals parading in a field of human activity, in an abyss of mutual ambiguities, mutual accommodations where the victims of the exposed and entangled state remain, keeping up the complexity of the grounds."

Aunt Mildred grabbed the full implications of an identity whose sense of immediacy depends on a state of temporal abeyance.

Property

"The period between the hyphen of marriage is best forgotten," said her uncle, salivating at the gate of that boundless menagerie primed with a moral shape which is framed to break down on approach to vivid fact. The property was neglected. A label peeled away from a jar in a city under cloudless skies. Anybody in the center of the meadow where the cows stand still, where rivers spit and salt subdues the perspicacity of skin with humdrum metabolic flowering diminishing the general regard for this miscellaneous Hector while staring at one's own face through a deserving mirror, might hold to her bosom the happy halting view of this interesting case.

MURDERING

AS SOON AS THE FLAME TOOK UP THE LAST WORD AND AGAIN IN the darkness that muted cry the stone began to turn inside another enclosed place resembling a trumpet or the broken membrane in the hearing of an old skunk singing and singing through the funnel of an instrument wearing a tux reflecting a little scene-stealer staring at dross. For she was indeed staring at dross and nothing could gather any others' attention than the two bows bending parallel with color that she had theatrically staged herself as. She entreated Juno as if she were not surrounded by department stores consumed like the sun, with vapors. And this is what she said, "Oh, Juno. Every code of honor is a code of torture. Every move I make outside the house is taken to be theatrical. I have never been able to truly act the drama that is myself or that I am in because everything has already been assigned to me as theater. Even walking down the street is staged. But now I have taken drama, as if it were the law, into my own hands, as if you and I together arrived at the time of the making of our parents.

And so she, they, doubled, the goddess and the staged effect, looked on from within the valley of that canto where their parents had been born.

They found the parents lying in a quiet passage at opposite ends of an abandoned highway tunnel. This was the birthing house of common folk. Their guide said, "Each came into the world enclosed in a silence close to death, long before you became their daughters."

These daughters, this goddess and this staged effect, were becoming aware, gradually of an alternative environment that seemed to be imposing itself on them, beginning at the ceiling where light of an artificial nature braided in and out of the eternal scene with an overwrought glow. They recalled something they had learned in a school for nice girls meant to end-up-right-where-they-started, about merchandise and the balance between asking too much and not enough of one's stocks. Yes, warehoused merchandise had begun to spill onto the floor.

Juno and the staged effect had been standing next to the buffet in the basement of the department store without recognizing the disappearance of their primal valley scene. Now, trapped by hundreds of half-pint milk cartons crowding the floor, they could not imagine how to get out of the jumble, which had been degraded further by the collapse of woolen sweaters from somewhere overhead onto the milk cartons. Juno and the staged effect were up to their knees in the processed residues of cows and sheep with their analytical powers suspended in a netherworld between what once was and what comes next.

At once it became clear to the guide that the birthing place was not real. The staged effect had, with the help of her own twisted charm, simply painted a picture for the goddess representing the moment of their parents' birth. She'd picked the idea up from the place she wouldn't say she was from and couldn't be traced to without some other responsible party getting involved. The guide stood on that brink called hesitation.

He knew what his employer could not articulate, that his sex and his way of life were as one.

Juno and the staged effect, oblivious of this recuperative surveyor known as guide, faced off this time before the muted flame like people who have been under masks and seem other than before. The guide was oblivious to the difference between this and any other moment in their surging acquaintance.

In fiction, murder is the inverse of murder in life. In fiction, murder occurs with great regularity, holding down a symbolic order known as plot. If all the murders in fiction were wiped out, perhaps something sexier and messier would take their place. For murder is the cleanest thing in fiction, even if a filthy thing in life.

ANIMAL INSTINCTS

1

OUT *MY* WINDOW THE VIEW BLOCKS WHAT'S BEHIND IT. THIS WOULD not be true for Balzac, who had a photographic memory.

In any case, I know that the village is neither square nor long, that science has special status in private life, and that no one is aware of anyone's standards. Here the road forks and the mind cannot advance.

Perhaps this is the reason, or excuse, for my biography. Privacy may be caught out on a limb, but one can backtrack through endless plagiarisms to a fictional era, pure discourse that can be imitated, that can take advantage of modern life.

We enjoy the humor of the sun since it contributes

to our prosperity. It is nearly impossible to be lonely. And if someone out on the drive sneaks through the lips of a jacaranda pouncing on your ideologies inside, never fear. Ideologies are useful scavengers in their clearing of debris (see the body dancing without the head?) from the mind, and civilized only to that extent.

A crane is stopping at a tomato patch.

It has passed now. Everything is intended to amuse. That is why nothing lasts. Economy does not enter the picture; the pile in the center is water in mid-thrust, pointing a finger as in a Disney cartoon. Transformation being more strategic than logic, all this must be true.

If the town got the results it wanted, everything would be squared away. Desert and herds of animals enter: the narrative traffic rhymes in the bullpen of great events. They'll screw 'em every time, says a traitor to progress, but maybe that's all right. Heretofore neglected stalls will be brimming with hay.

Eat this, eat that. Yes, I will have some, thank you.

For a detective, I am an unusual person. I am using the crime to make myself understood. (Perhaps not so unusual at that.) This is what was attractive about Poe's detectives. They stayed in the house and people came to them. Unfortunately those people were either self-important or self-effacing. They wanted to erase excitement down to the marrow of their bones. Bravura was employed to arouse the detective's interest in the case. If resistance did not exist neither would bravura. Obviously things have changed.

Also, I am not a tidy person.

I am standing under a palm wearing my green hat and matching jacket, holding a walking stick. A man and a woman are also standing under the palm. I am repulsed by this tourism—exclusive of the fact that they are what we are. *Some* of us scrutinize the mistrust we feel emanating from the others. I would not be doing this if I were not getting paid.

I am strapped with the space where there is no rest. Various incidents occur to me, trail into my line of work and keep me in a continually wavering state. When you see that everything is interconnected the imagination will up and randomize. Wan features of the bared chest, the balloon blown up around a gun.

I am told that I am as simple as an animal with an animal's simple ignorance of right and wrong, dislike for being thwarted, and spitefulness when trapped. I take it as a compliment and let it go at that. A moralism of which the literal content was superior to Spade's understanding.

On the balcony, under a tree, behind the window.

(Madame Feuzele-Lace poured herself some tea and waited for her English husband to return to Flanders. She had been waiting, oh, a decade, with a sentinel at her door, an odd bird, who reminded the occasional visitor of a flamingo about to rise from the pages of one of Monsieur Lace's exotic books. Madame Feuzele-Lace, on the other hand, resembled an owl. She staggered in daylight like a midwife who had known countless sleepless days and nights. And her bookcases, once the meticulously ordered, cherished objects of her husband's pride, *elles ont été dans le pétrin.* They might as well have been chicken coops, so randomly were they littered with books—and the books, the books might as well have been feed! Thus would exclaim the occasional visitor while rattling on to a neighbor.

It was acknowledged by all that Madame Feuzele's—her name was often shortened in favor of the French—acquaintance was relished as a remarkable conquest, indeed.

At night Madame Feuzele seemed to comprehend everything that had evaded her understanding during the day. She had a prototypically Balzacian dichotomy embedded in her nature. Her servants shied away from her while walking through the house with their cats.

The servant Lily was educated, but Madame Feuzele didn't know this. Lily made use of her education to command the others.

Like a new machine, the household entered the day with chrome-plated coos and danced on its springs till bedtime. Even so, Madame Feuzele was in a perpetual state of spiritual crisis since she was unable to determine whether or not anything in her yard, the village, the country, or the world had changed, or if it had not, if it would, someday, in her lifetime. Her obsessive pensiveness was bound to present Monsieur with an odd kettle of fish, if he were ever to return, which he fully intended to do, after he had rid himself of the disgrace that had forced him to flee the suburbs of Paris so many years ago.)

This story will be cast into eternity. It will never exist. Lily has the key to all the rooms in the chateau and is running through the corridors in her bare feet.

One lingers, envisioning oneself as a link in a missing chain. There must be some kind of magnetic attraction to the weeping willow draped over stagnant water; some ultramannerism encourages a dragnet of espionage over the swans fighting for the muddy bank.

Yes, the superannuated plover of melodrama is about to grow fins. The shape that was lacking is revealed. An orangutan holds her ground with outthrust arms. She has gravity before she has desire.

Because of animal instincts, I am not an epigrammatic thinker. Every being that matures gets caught up in problems of interpretation. To be sure, I have given in to a slight impulse to dismiss this case, to walk beyond the palms into a garden of buried arrows and stick my head in a trough. Then I change my mind because I could never be that primitive. I cling to the subject at hand as if I were the specimen.

The film (is it a film?) has gone off course. I say slide and the picture tilts. I, the audience, strangle a volcano. It chokes, sputters, and thousands are saved. Then a train in Java has stopped at a village and the passengers are invited to get out and look for eggs. Time has been put to the side. We are not allowed to inspect the racks of meat until after we have dined, but I can't tell if my desire to examine them, especially the rabbits and chickens, has to do with hunger that has now been satisfied, or federal (or international?) employment. I am trailing the Périphérique. The market is a place where the person I want won't go. Some other name is in operation. This person is sheltered by a casino. Chandeliers, hanging from magnetic vats, subdue the tabula rasa as the entourage stencils monuments with hidden hands. They clear the road with onions. There's a premium on good manners. As I make my resolution to embrace literalmindedness, the Kalahari Desert produces a street—on which one is either a buyer or a seller. I have nothing to sell and no money but would eat joyfully the tinkling bells, the pleasurable scene. Obviously I am a suspicious character since I have nothing to do, no insignia to divine. The sun is so warm.

Take that Aladdin's lamp away!
But you asked to see it, sir.
I asked to see a map, can't you understand English?
A little; *mais je parle français.*
What are you doing here in that case? Mister Lace never intended to get into these kinds of conversations, but he was so demanding he ended up paying the price of having to listen to others justify their existence.
I study *la médecine* at night.
Well, you never can tell, can you? Perhaps you'll turn into a great doctor.

Bien, Monsieur. I have just begun to understand the throat. The esophagus . . .
I'm so frustrated I'd like to take this sarcophagus and cram it down someone's gullet. I should have been born a soldier of fortune. After all, I live worse. That's an idea you know, I could go into business making chocolate coffins.
Monsieur, here we have a particularly compelling map.
Map crap. This place is making me break out in hives. Where are we anyway?
We are just this side of the Atlantic.
You are a very foolish boy.

2

I am under the influence of (someone's saying be softer, kinder, less direct) bassoons. In this metropolis, a century listens before it is heard. The choir loft is on the ground because of delusions of paradise. At this time of day the world turns gold. I have a marvelous view of rosebushes. Nothing is happening, the gate opens or closes, I have no desire to meet anyone, the solitude is exact, etc.

What is the image of a solitary figure I wish to defeat?

The sun, humanly speaking (it is mentioned so often that it is confused with the notion of midday) is the most exalted conception. It is also the greatest abstraction, because it is impossible to fix on it at any hour.

At one moment my mind relaxes filled with the vision, on the screen, of pastel. The next second I see that I have been the butt of a joke, for we are now in an earlier century and being led to the executioner. A white donkey pulls a cart over one of the dusty hills surrounding the town. Then the axe catches the sun and glitters. It is not pleasant to be alive anyway. One dwells on this revelation for a very long time in order to determine its validity and while doing this misses most of the crowd shots. It is now too late to study the expressions of the people in the crowd.

This meditation is instigated by the recollection of numerous images of priests. The duty of the priest is to elaborate on the purpose, function, and consequences of sinning to the criminal. Here one notes that at certain moments to be descriptive is to be rotten. The priest is a public figure and on such occasions has very few means at his disposal to show compassion. He must find a way to let the criminal know that he really is human and is treating his own priestly intonations ironically. Without anyone observing his transgression, the priest shows kindness with compassionate eyes and knowing looks while indulging in the excesses of speech. But one is always left in doubt as to the true intentions of such a public figure, since on the subject of personal motives he is compelled to remain mute. It is impossible to believe finally that a condemned person has been comforted in the end.

3

(Madame Feuzele-Lace loved the semblance of order but hated its reality. She memorized her escape route then tore up the map and threw it into the fireplace. She flew to the servants' rooms in search of twigs.

Physiologists and profound observers will tell you, perhaps, to your great astonishment, that tempers, characteristics, wit, or genius reappear in families at long intervals, precisely like what are known as hereditary diseases. Madame Feuzele was reported to be a somnambulist and a magnetizer in search of the Philosopher's Stone.

Had she never stolen a twig, the plush forest would still grieve outside while she was inside warming herself, imagining herself a tree. The sky moved to the end of a serpent, changing the dirt to grey. She thought then of her reality. Me, I am only a name, but the trees address the one who is me and not a name. She tried to remember her husband's face but nothing remained of him in her heart.

The sight of upturned soil makes every creature avid and watchful; Lily would have preferred to have nothing to do with the fate of Madame Feuzele. And why she had to sense what no one had asked her to sense, galled her.

Eyes kept open guard against the forceful personality. If one has contemplated violating a social pact and is beaten to the violation by another whose nerves have been trodden to minutiae by habitual compliance, what can one see in a mirror? It was clear to Lily that Madame Feuzele was intending to become Lily.

Lily was not so sure that she was going to take the opportunity to become Madame Feuzele, but it had occurred to her, as Madame scurried around the chateau like a rat, that she, Lily, could sell some of the farmland surrounding the chateau without anyone suspecting that she was not Madame Feuzele . . .

She looked in the mirror. She too had a rodent lodged there, but hers was cute and wiggled its ears, a wise little rodent barrier to the truth. She closed her eyes and spotted the rabbit in the middle of a long, hot road. The insipid thing had its easel out and was perkily painting the ominous forest that came up to the road on one side. On the other side were orchards, cornfields, and meadows with crows. There were also a number of broken statues as one approached the chateau.

The faster one draws, the longer one rolls in the surf, the more agilely one congeals and disperses standards of any sort with or without equipment, the neater one hides one's hair, and so on to the end of a row of infringements, the more graceful the shape of any old thing becomes to a witness. Lily lacked speed and the agility to spot, to move, to draw without burdening herself with meaning.

The stone limbs that ornamented the meadow, narcissi and iris sprouting between open fingers and nestling in crooked arms, or the bent knee of an Orpheus under the surveillance of a drooping digitalis, these charming insignia might caress the workman, spy, the uninvited traveler into an observation. What this estate lacks in maintenance it compensates for in honesty, a naive professional says to the open mind gliding through the meadow.

But to Lily, whose every breath renews an alter ego, some Constance, the open spaces take on the significance of duplicates; the photograph is a mannerism of what's left out. The puppets on land are controlled by the hidden Constance.)

Sometimes people dream they are in love, with no one. Dresses hang in the closet opening onto a garden. Let us ascend from the lab: the gates of the future open, but this gelatinous world exists only in relation to a missing subject. You look for the one thing, but fringe grows between you and where your boat's been launched. One could search the world or never leave the library and get the same results.

It is time to return to discipline.

Enter Flea, followed by Radio.

There are usually one or two people in the balcony who scrutinize such absurdities for symbolism because the person wearing the flea is an actor, known to them. What is intended to be sequential is stratified. God walks on, whipping an antelope in order to add an element of criminality to the pretend activity of seasonal mating and self-denial behind a superficial if not spurious maze of doors, most of them painted on, not functional, but this friend, interpreter, the "plant" thinks that the god is meant to be some god, and that he gets what he's after offstage. The pity of it all, these plants have managed a gleam of truth!

However, a plant could also be thinking something else quite different, could be drowning in humility from what's hinted at in an exchange of lines:

—Sorry, Harry, you'll have to pull down the circus and start over.

—I didn't want it to turn out this way, Sue.

Could be dying while the figures on stage call each other by name with confounding ease, with each other's failings in hand. The contrast between plant and character is so great that the result is extreme self-deception. Hence, the problem with superficial intelligence is that it is unhappy with itself. And as a consequence it finds meaning to be overflowing.

Enough said. So much for making points, fishing for broken glass. The blank magnolias bow to all forgetfulness. Rose petals fall from the sky.

(A few minutes later all the personages of this domestic drama are once more united in the drawing room, surprised to see Lily sitting by a man, flirting with him in the best style of the most wily Parisienne. The man is none other than Monsieur Lace, who has, essentially, just stepped off the boat. He cannot tack down the rationale for his speech, due, he thinks, to the surprise of finding himself at home with a servant after what he now gaily calls his exile.

It was a self-imposed sentence, he says.

The vague outlines of a unifying principle appear to support his opacity. Lily watches the ghosts from his past as he unwittingly announces their presence.

People believed I was a bad man for not enjoying myself, so I flew the coop in search of pleasure.

I dare not ask if you succeeded.

Whatever anyone thinks, I am not an evil man.

I will not pursue the question for fear that I will be thought an evil woman.

You? Evil?

Lily responds, dramatizing wildly flailing her arms as if she were trying to charm Satan: I have been shut in with your wife for many years. I have paced the halls and anxiously dusted the furniture twice daily. Each day I have stood on the brink of what seemed to be doom, as if about to be roped into an undesired marriage, or as if the world outside this house were a labyrinth of dungeons. Here, inside, this darkness and dankness served as light, for I believed the meadows on all sides would turn into roaring furnaces if I stepped onto them. When I tried to rid myself of this anxiety, I was tricked out of it: to succeed, I would have had to rid Madame of her anxiety since it was hers that produced mine, mine that tricked her into believing in her own, so that at some point there may have been no difference between us. But there was a difference. My anxiety was not motivated by grief. We were split apart like body and soul. The soul sits on the sofa, locked in place. The body twitches and moves helter-skelter over the brink of disaster performing the duties the soul has eclipsed. When something is missing there are two when there ought to be one. Now that you have returned there is nothing left.

But I'm here, says Mr. Lace.

It is not the real you. You have been stripped of motivation. You are here to obey.

Am I alive?

You are half alive.

Lily withdrew her mask, and Madame Feuzele emerged: she tipped her head slightly upward so that her husband could see her radiant glow, the result of her impeccable deception.)

4

A hole in the Pyrenees can have nothing in common with a hole in the Outback.

They were on a journey. They were making holes in the snow, then moving on and digging holes in canyons, on alluvial fans next to plants that resembled brains. Everyone likes to hear about their journey to Antarctica and to Australia. They slept in the pouches of kangaroos. They were emanations of the future. And as we know, the future is in the hands of anything or anyone. If the future were the same for everyone and everything this would mean the end of the world.

No one knows if anything ever grew inside their diggings. In the hands of culture, meaning multiplies, drifts away from creation, blows ambiguity out of proportion and enslaves it. We could relativize by surmising anything in particular and relieve the earth of its pressure. But the physical dimension of this story is unexplored. There is not one photograph of a shoe; no tattered shirts remain, no speech to fill up the mystery.

Inexplicable phenomena are made up by the people who witness them rather than those who cause them. One would have you perceive her to be a thinker. But in order for her to know what she thought, she had to ask her mother to debunk the books and bats. The mother, who could not help but do anything for the child, considered herself a failure precisely because of this helplessness; the cat climbed all over the stars. She charmed posterity. And One judged her. One chose between weak and strong alternately; for she understood that it was important to have fragile views that could give way under stress to unrelated subjects. Water evaporates, then the baby uses the empty container to shovel sand. Whereas tightwad views efface the panorama. One was continually adjusting her map, which was made of large crusty pieces, and playing for hours in her messy abstraction. At some point the walls could not accommodate all the adjustments and One had to go out into the world. In all respects Two followed One.

Everyone but Two, who was the slave to One, recognized Two's special character. When One was calculating, Two, who had no need to calculate since One was doing that, would record One's thoughts. Then everybody would laugh. Two loved the humor in others without recognizing that her own wit was the specialty of the house. People would jump from high windows because Two's unself-consciousness exasperated even the plants. She was opaque and unpliable in drastic situations because she graciously followed the leader. She was gasping for air, having no use for discussion. Consequently there was no way out for Two and there was no way into Two for One, that is anyone. This made Two in old age hopelessly lonely.

What this consorority had to do with *Play Q* I wasn't sure. The thumb on my desk was certainly mine, and I had been staring at it for hours without seeing it. Finally I noticed my hand and that the thumb and hand were joined. I was back in my own skin in time to escape a case of the horrors. I went to the garage and found my car after about ten minutes. I knew the crumbling house would fall with or without my attention. I turned right on M Street feeling like a squirrel in a healthy pine.

When I pulled up I couldn't believe my eyes. The shack was narrow and split in half. I got out of the car and walked around. What I found was some organizational propaganda.

The general atmosphere was distinctly unfamiliar. The window through which the distracting light of centuries flooded a quasi-dingy room, wandered in its hinges. The ground was soft. There was no next time, but there were stepping stones. All detail half warm, half cold. In the trees, loud jays sweetened these divisions.

FAIRY TALE

A LITTLE GIRL, GROWING UP IN THIS STORY IS AS THRILLED BY THIS world as any well loved and well fed child would be in any other story. She lives in Iraq. In a city. Her mother is an engineer. One day, the girl is picking up her toys and singing on the porch. It is dry and hot but a storm cloud is up there. When everyone goes inside for dinner, the girl stays outside, on the porch, observing the cloud. It descends and speaks to her. "I don't want to scare you, says the cloud. But listen. Do not worry about me. But protect your mother." What am I to do?" asks the child. The storm cloud answers, "Someday the mendacious ones will come to your city and they will try to destroy it but not all the way only part way, their way so they can say that "it is not destroyed," and they will be saying something true and false at the same time. They will tell you they are dividing good from bad. The good people from the bad. The good weapons from the bad. The good governments from the bad. And they will take all of the resources and try to give them to the good people and they will try to destroy all the bad people's resources. Now it is obvious that they conflate right and wrong, good and bad and even make up right and wrong good and bad in order to duplicate to infinity their duplicity, but no one knows whether or not they can really tell the good from the bad or if they are just making it up. This causes much controversy, which they also use to their advantage, by duplicating their duplicity all over the world while everybody argues about what they know and what they don't know. They are parasites on controversy, and some even say that controversy to them is like food to us, and that they come from another world that surrounds our world, one we can't see, and that they feed off us in every way imaginable and even in some ways that are not imaginable." "Stop!" says the child. "Okay," says the cloud, "but never say the word good or the word bad and you will save your mother." The furious child throws down her toys. Blasted against the house by child fury, the toys slip into little heaps. The cloud moves away, the sky looks gradually lighter then washed, even scrubbed. The child gathers her toys around her and sings to them and the sunlight warms them.

One day, the child begins to notice that many things are assigned the word good and many things are assigned the word bad. Sometimes, something that is assigned the word good on one day is assigned the word bad on another day. She notices that sometimes people are said to be good and at other times they are said to be bad. And that often the same person will be an object in a fluctuating judgment; a judgment, that although it fluctuates, has no memory. Only contemporaneity.

One day, an oil-stained seabird slides to her porch. Poking its ochre beak in her face it says, "where is your good mother?" The stains on its back hold a gruesome code. From them, she divines the seabird ransacking the house and poking out her mother's eyes. Swept all over with fear, the child flees to the kitchen then returns with shrimps in a packet, which she throws at the bird. "My mother? My mother is this," she whispers nearly choking on her words. But the bird disappears in a flame, surrounded by soft evening light. The street fills with voices, dinner aromas, and people coming and going.

By now, the encounter with the bird has become a wonderful memory for the child who believes she has saved her mother and seen magic at work too. But why did it want to see mother? She knows that in some countries mothers can only be seen in certain places. Was it a custom she was following in not letting the bird see her mother? On this present day, a strange soldier comes to her house. The girl is playing with her toys on the porch. "Are you the bad little girl who stole our excuse for existence?" he asks as if he were asking for a cube of ice. She thinks this is the strangest question she has ever heard. "I am only a girl," she says, and the strange soldier goes away. The girl watches him walking down the street poking his gun into doorways.

The mendacious sycophants play a big trick on everybody in her known world. When war breaks out as a result and the city and the people are randomly destroyed by enormous bombs, the cloud again confronts the girl.

"Remember," says the cloud. She remembers her father who died in the last war. Again she is swept with fear as if little fear particles were flying into her, igniting in her. The cloud disappears. Every day with bombs coming randomly down from the sky, she looks up into the sky for the cloud. It is as if the whole world hates her city. Or her. It is as if everybody she's ever seen is hated by everybody else she has never seen. What have we done? She looks into the sky, she looks for the cloud, she says what have we done? But she resists saying that anything is either good or bad.

She calls the water water and the sky sky and people people. She calls agriculture and nature agriculture and nature, music music and silence silence, the Kurds, the Palestinians, the Turks, the Jewish, the Muslims, the Christians, the Kurds, the Palestinians, the Turks, the Jewish, the Muslims, the Christians, she calls a cloud a cloud. She calls the mendacious sycophants something oblique and imagines them as a line running to infinity. Do they have mothers and fathers? What made them? She draws lines in the sand with her finger on her way to school and imagines the lines wrapping around the world and going out to infinity. She walks in a line she calls infinity with one foot setting itself perfectly before the next. She walks with a feeling of power over the wind that blows the fragments from explosions hither and yon. If the school is not there when she arrives, she will return home to her mother, who will be there, as long as she remains vigilant. Even if it is the end of the world. She calls the end of the world the end of the world until it evaporates like a line in a song. And recurs like a line in a song.

She divines the following when studying the miscellaneous fragments from exploded things arranged in patterns in the road, on the sand on her way to school: that the power that creates the mendacious sycophants must be the same thing as the end of the world. She begins to imagine the end of the world. Because she will not think about good and bad, and sometimes not even now those images one might associate with good and bad, even though those images are objectified all around her, she imagines this power that creates the end of the world to be without boundaries, without taste, or texture or smell. It is entirely neutral. A reverse order entirely neutral with the words "the end of the world" echoing mechanically, as if from a machine producing a stuck fact. And so it has already come. It is a finite point stuck on a line, on the other side of which are some other words. Or is she only being hopeful? Or it, again, the same thing, again, like a stuck song. She throws everything in her arms down and runs home, where her mother is working, leaning over some paper. She grabs her mother with great force, around the legs, and rubs her face into her mother's belly, having survived the worst and the best outcome, given the circumstances.

In a fairy tale it is important that all the circumstances are understood.

—not the end—

MEMBERSHIP

THEY PLACED THEIR DEMENTED MUSINGS OUTSIDE THEMSELVES, and called the displacement society and public space. Therefore, society and public space were the projected fantasies of individuals onto the ground we once occupied. A room in the "public realm" looked like a demand in a very loud voice, with a hidden threat waiting behind its vocalizations. "Public" structures were indeed the facsimile resulting from fantasies of demented fanatics with excess power: the institutions all had to be negotiated around, within, between this way and that in a continuum of daily maneuverings. Most negotiations involved avoiding the institutions as much as possible. Why should a few fanatics absorb the wild fantasies of the *rest-of-us* was a common complaint against "public participation," as defined by the institutions. But some, like electrons, struck the projected wave of institutionality at the right moment, just as a door had opened, or a window of opportunity. This was counted on by the handful of creators: 10,000 in a million would bounce at the right moment into the projected wave and be welcomed inside as participants. What did they do inside?

Sometimes news from these institutions bounced out as if quantums of energy given off during a hidden event. Because of the dearth of information surrounding these leaked quantums of news, they became significant. The news became huge, magnified as it was in the field-glasses of silent fears. Through magnified fear, the "outside" got a glimmer of what it was like to be entered into the institution. The pieces of news, once leaked, became giant spectacles, hurling their flag-torn and lock-ridden bodies into tea houses, book stalls and other randomly concocted enterprises.

How could a quantum have provoked such a break in the routine life, which consisted of avoidance of the "public good" as prescribed by the projections of a handful of lunatics who think of their creations as the determinants of society?

Because there was no other way, no other realm than this realm of negative positivity and positive negativity, all were always already gathered around these projected institutions, even in their avoidance of them. Those who had been institutionalized and those who had shirked imprisonment, all made up a reciprocating form of knowledge.

Now that we have achieved happier circumstances, we can tip our hats in gratitude to those ancient ones who could only act on their knowledge of imprisonment and freedom by doing something together that pleased them within and without the institutional walls. From them, we learned the sacrament of specific pleasures, such as tease parties, and other things the smallest unit of measurable energy has not been known to be able to achieve on its own.

MEGHOM

NOT EVERYTHING ANYONE EVER WANTED TO SAY CAN FIT HERE.
Piles of excess are heaped at the borders.

This is the game of minute resistance. Do not try to
imagine how small but just keep minute resistance in mind.
Doing so will appropriately limit your actions and you will be
a viable player.

You can play with others or by yourself. There is usually a motive for playing. A no symbolically related to a quantum no, a grand enfoldment of no. This small no, this no is
symbolically related is what you are playing with. It is in the
scale of meghom, and it has a life of its own. You, too have a
life of your own.

Many of us are playing this game inside the Utopian

Borders. It is not illegal: it is not too small to be noticed. When playing, it is important to remember the words, **the scale of minute resistance**. If you become bored with the repetitions in this description of playing, you may skip. You do not have to be told to skip.

Sometimes there are drugs on the playing field, but they are not part of the game.

Sometimes there are arguments on the playing field, but they are not part of the game.

Sometimes there are weapons on the playing field, but they are not part of the game.

The intention of the game is to invisibly shift history without the sources of the shift being identified and without the shift being understood as history. It will not be seen through an historical record or theory, but it nevertheless affects the outcome of the record or the theory without the recorders or theorizers knowing.

Sometimes there is an affair on the playing field, and although affairs are not within the boundaries of the game, an affair may activate a move in the game if it has no perceptible effect on the world and no one ever learns about it—not even in historical time.

When playing the game of minute resistance, it is important to watch out for the deities of minute effects. They are as small as the smallest actions, and they can infiltrate your intentions. When your intentions become deified, you are out.

Changing memory to notoriety may be within the bounds of the game if no one notices.

Intentional negligence such as handing someone a dull pencil or arguing for one thing and then another, contradictorily, without anyone noticing can count.

No one will notice if you refuse, quietly, to fully grasp each sentence in this document or any document. In fact, you can tell when a statesman/woman is *not* playing the game for they will announce their need to fully grasp something that has been spoken or read, and you will know that this is not true, that the words **fully grasp** coming out of their mouths, in fact, mean **delete what I don't want to know**. The phrase **fully grasp** is an announcement of resistance, an assertion that overtly conceals the desire to resist information.

To resist information and play the game you have to know you are resisting and not let anybody else know, ever.

A glorious woman sits on top of a pile on the border of the playing field of Meghom. She is laughing. "These small crimes are so easy to get away with," she says. She laughs more. The people on the playing field admire her.

But she is not on the playing field.

Sometimes she may even tell you she is getting away with a crime as she announces and commits it. No one, she says, can see, and yet I am taking what is not mine in front of your very eyes. But this is not the game. It is the expression of a superficial and counterproductive sentiment derived from an insatiable desire to enter the fray.

MARGIN

Who Do You Think You Are?

patent number sx 900-1

Description: the game board itself is blank. The game comes with a set of transparencies of a size equal to the game board, which one places on top of it. The transparencies are titled *Who Do You Think You Are?: Error Game Board. Who Do You Think You Are?: Correction Game Board. Who Do You Think You Are?: Normal Game Board. Who Do You Think You Are?: Citizenship Game Board. Who Do You Think You Are?: Love/Outcast Game Board. Who Do You Think You Are?: Error Game Board Fictional Specialty* or *Who Do You Think You Are?: Religious/Outcast Game Board Pre-Christian Specialty* or *St. Ignatious Catholic Schools Specialty.* In this way, the product marketing can hit all its targets. The basic transparency is simply overlaid with a specialty that adds to its density.

Subsets, on the other hand, can be applied to all basic game board transparencies. They add details to the game by increasing the margin layer; so, for instance, if one were playing a game from the *Basic Set*, one would circulate around a narrow margin, but if a subset transparency were added, the margin would thicken toward the center. However, as we all know, the center is always empty. We would never be able to agree on anything without this basic concept, much less the rules of a board game

Pure Products of America, Blind Alley, Roller Coaster, Feuds, Exploitation, Cooking, Women Only, Men Only, Kids Only, Pioneers—of science, of preserving traditions, of education, of the wilderness, of civil rights (whatever can be found in newspaper headings)—are some of the subsets that can be applied to any of the games in the *Basic Set*. Can one play a game with a subset and a specialty? Yes.

One of the most popular among adults is the *Love/ Outcast Game Board Outer Space Specialty* with a *Pure Products of America Subset*. It appeals to more than one side of personal desire. It might be obvious that younger adults might prefer *Love/Outcast Game Board Outer Space Specialty with Roller Coaster Subset*.

One premise of the game is that most people perceive themselves as marginalized. There are potential players in almost all markets. In the '80s, for instance, you could, if you had the right job, overhear rich people moaning and groaning about having too much money. When I learned that they were truly disturbed that they were losing money because they had too much, I decided that there is a possibility that all civilization is built on the expectation of, or desire for, marginality. Excuse me for inserting myself into this blueprint. Authors, I understand, are not the voice behind their own games; however, a personal touch could be satisfying when it provides the sensation that products originate in something or someone.

Sometimes one is very much in need of knowing what other people think; the *Citizenship Game Board* may be consulted. Why? I will return to that later. Many people want to use the game as pure entertainment. Do they avoid the *Citizenship Game Board?* If they are citizens? If they have green cards? If they are illegal immigrants? One survey indicates that adult immigrants tend to give away this transparency to nieces and nephews trying to master the Constitution.

The truth of the matter is the *Citizenship Game Board* holds many secrets: it constitutes and develops secrets. You will not find many government immigration bureaucrats in diamond-patterned ties and purple silk dresses playing *Who Do You Think You Are Citizenship Game Board* on their days off. But wander into someone's work cubicle and see if they haven't wedged an extra table against the file cabinet with the potted succulent that hasn't been watered for five months on top, see if on that table there isn't a game board transparency with state of-the-art "remote tokens."

It is not clear what will happen next.

Curiously, these people are of the very few who do not seem to see themselves as on the margin. But sometimes when you meet the eye of one of these bureaucrats, you see a soft cry, a "Don't leave me out." Then you learn that they are being paid to maintain a certain appearance, one of belonging to a group that everybody else recognizes as the group into which one is supposed to assimilate. Of course, if you are very rich this is repulsive: that silk dress was never in fashion, nor the mediocre education and poor appreciation of culture, the government cafeteria and so on.

Models stick but to what?

This bureaucrat is only a stereotype who investigates the legitimacy of aliens, who studies the future flood of illegal immigration by playing this game: *Who Do You Think You Are?: Citizenship/Illegal Alien Specialty.* And now the stereotype begins to investigate who the illegal alien thinks she is.

It is a good question who she is. The sounds the illegal alien has never heard before are reminiscent of new drugs taking effect. She is almost ridiculed by the high-pitched wail of a jay imitating a hawk as she reaches the ruby land spreading above the obscure seaport bluff she has just finished climbing. She creeps into a panic as a plane passes overhead. Soon others like her will follow her, clogging up these narcotic effects of landscape retribution with more familiar noise.

Back in the office, our stereotype dials the number listed in the manual. She speaks to the game guide on the other end of the line, "Do you have any *Motives Subsets?* Or *Motivation Specialties?* **You** want more information from **me?** Well, I'm an immigration specialist and I don't understand your *Citizenship Game.* Your games aren't meant for experts? But you claim they're meant for everybody!"

The inner voice of the bureaucrat screams silently, "Everybody but me!"

Are there people who spend all of their time leaving other people out? Or is this "just a game?"

Let me in!

The answer is yes. The token advances by remote.

Sometimes tokens advance, depending on the game, only when the answer is yes.

It is possible to play alone.

It is possible to adapt the game to the computer, but this won't happen in the near future, because people enjoy the blank board, the layering of the board with transparencies. You don't have to have a token to know where you are, but some use them and stereotypes always enjoy the remotes.

Some people, such as those stuck on American naval bases on the tip of Cuba have no interest in the adaptability of this game to other media. They are experiencing a depletion that even goes beyond the boundaries of the narrowest margins of *Who Do You Think You Are?*

MACARTHUR (MIMESIS)

The game question is: *Is the following a representation of General MacArthur?*

CONCLUSION: *The shot of a traffic light held too long is no longer a traffic light.*

HYPOTHESIS: However, General MacArthur, his head obscured, his legs cut off and the representation of his garb tinted with pink pockets, *is* General MacArthur.

BACKGROUND: There is nowhere to go. There is nowhere to develop. War heroes games are all over the minute they get off the boat. To play a game called General MacArthur one must re-create where he went and what he did before he got off the boat.

QUESTION: And if one traces the history of the replication of General MacArthur?

FICTION: For the last time General MacArthur paces up and down. General MacArthur is happy as a clam. General MacArthur's power has been unleashed and reassigned by strangers to defeat him and his white compatriots. An infinity of traffic lights opposes the eternity of the General.

CONCLUSION: When the camera is held too long on the General he enters infinity.

RESIDUE: Only the dreck of General MacArthur is stationed in the boat hold. Only allies play the game General MacArthur. Where he went and what he did is re-created. Children learn the story from sailors, whom they mock later as old jokes.

QUESTION: Does mimesis domesticate the arbitrary? Does mimesis reinvest the arbitrary with power? Does mimesis arbitrate power? Do the reproductions of General MacArthur domesticate his power? Do the reproductions of General MacArthur parade an automatism outside his power? In calling up General MacArthur, does one reclaim an original investment in power?

JOURNALISM: General MacArthur disembarks. General MacArthur walks on the shore. General MacArthur enters history.

FAIRY TALE: Once upon a time, General MacArthur took care of our people. Every night we turned off our lights. The memory of light gave us a fact: Hiroshima.

POETRY: The carved reproduction of the General is protection against the General. Inside the General is pacing walls of granite. What is in the mind of the person who sees the general as inside himself pacing walls of granite? MacArthur is geographic eternity, obviously: but the obvious is never obvious to him in his boat moored on southern shores, above *all that anchors history*.

HYPOTHESIS: In the geographic eternity of imagination, changes in habitats happen over night, in one fell swoop and beyond our wildest dreams.

HABITAT: Inside the wooden replication of General MacArthur is a soul. It is not his soul; therefore, when the old sailors tell children about the time they saw General MacArthur, the geographic eternity of distant shores close the history books. Eyes close to books.

CONCLUSION: From a distance, history argues against this superficial and willful act of amnesia. When he was a child, Napoleon saw that he was Napoleon.

MIMESIS: When the children play warfare they use updated missiles. They build walls and aim at a cubicle on the right side of the moon. They call themselves Captains Gabor and Babcock-Gutierrez. They inact the conditions of geographic eternity, the destruction of habitats overnight, clamoring in one fell swoop to recreate the wildest dreams.

MAGIC (OR ROUSSEAU)

IN ORDER TO PLAY, ONE NEEDS MAGIC AND ROUSSEAU AND MUST remember play. Sometimes magic is the obscurest impostor in play. An obscure rationalization imposes the word magic on Rousseau.

Now remember play has nothing to do with that Rousseauian freedom found in refusal.

Refusal more than anything else ends play.

And so we might play a game called the conjuring of Rousseau. It might go like this, let's pretend that Jean Jacques Rousseau is the pawn in our game. On one side of the board is society. On the other side of the board is solitude. We can each pick a goal. One of us tries to force Rousseau into society, the other tries to land him in solitude.

Whoever gets the pawn to the goal wins. Let's say Rousseau is walking along a Boulevard in silent reverie. The board, by the way, is made up of parks and boulevards, so when Rousseau "advances" he is always being advanced by way of a park or boulevard. Sometimes a player will draw a card that says, "What do you want Jean-Jacques Rousseau?" If the spinner lands on *I would like to go home,* then the pawn is returned to the beginning and Rousseau sets out again from the starting spot. If the spinner lands on *I would like to tell the truth,* the player gets to spin again until he gets something he likes; since truth is bound to both solitude and society, this move becomes a matter of preference. In the center of the board is a personage with great powers: she is a witch. If Jean-Jacques lands on her spot it is because she has called him up. She calls him up, because his travels fascinate her. Now, this is extremely problematic. If Rousseau realizes that she has called him up, then he sees himself as a ghost. The player has a choice at this point, to get out of or stay in the ghost game. If it is decided to stay in the ghost game, Rousseau is provided with a series of options that he never recognized when he was alive. He can, for instance, opt to infiltrate society without being noticed. He can observe those who outlived him. He could, if he were on the ladder to revenge, scare them to death. They could become equals in death. Or he could live with the witch, who loves to make good on her resources. This he admires enormously; although, she does not quite consider him her equal. With her, his solitude is indeed complete, since no one in the game believes in her existence.

THERE NEVER WAS A ROSE
WITHOUT A THORN[1]

Quantity

There is something absurd
There is nothing that stops. I am far

to myself spoiled . . . in 26 years, I

arriving in 4 hours
precisely

won't dine

It is not conditional
that the women will be obliging

all our hopes vanish

if we don't know
ignorance, is not more

than an object

don't you, me, when I
fuck you

and are we? Oh! heaven: you

Fixity

Have the biggest
fakers, forcefully

oppose yourselves

Ignorance is no longer an object
ten years minus

religion

Ignore us, no longer an object
all points are their erections

all

Not–France

I can't stuff myself anymore! (arguments in the form of noble people and ventriloquists seep out of the mortar of the chateau at the time of Louis XIV)

Death as observed by victims.

Death as observed by victims.

A death observed by a victim, death's victim. Something specific.

And so on.

Don't stop now.

Be as exact as possible.

Number four.

Number four! Death as observed.

Number five: In a theater, a piece of body rubbed on an erection.

More.

More.

Number six: Dies.

Number seven: The details, the details.

Number eight: Numbers take over the role of ventriloquists.

Number nine: A ventriloquist takes over the role of numbers: counting each hair as he pulls it out of his head.

Number 10: Dies.

Number 11: More.

Number 12: Another ventriloquist rises from the role of numbers and duplicates all previous actions, jerking the pecker of a nobleman every time he tears a hair out of his own head.

Number 13: A noblewoman announces the fall of the court of Louis XIV.

Number 15: Recount!

Number 16: Recount!

Number 17: Essay on redevelopment: the country. A number rips through the shirt of a noblewoman, who has announced the fall of the court from the stage. A ventriloquist grabs for the number which scissors through the woman's skirt and slinks into the woman's asshole just as the ventriloquist misses it. The ventriloquist. Is not protected.

Number 18: More detail.

Number 19: The ventriloquist plunges his hand into her ass and pulls it out screaming, minus a finger.

Number 20: The woman is consumed alive by the number cutting through her from the inside out.

Number 21: Announcement: death recounted by victims!

Number 22: As she dies, she is consumed by a heap of ventriloquists and numbers.

Number 23: Her sister is assigned to the task of making an encyclopedic account of the last day.

Number 24: The sister divides the day into days and the hours into days and the minutes into days and the seconds into days and the semi-seconds into days all of whom, once invented, judiciously enter her into the logos, the loges, or the lodge named Sade. He comes later.

Number 25: The foul residue of the court of Louis XIV march with provisions counted and recounted toothless, sewn shut, welted, and bored open to a gash in the middle of the condition that is Not–France.

The Origin of Not–France

In France

Our kitty Angel talks to Rousseau Raven, a paranoid she
loves, in her sleep. She says things to soothe him like

>Just say metamorphosis, it will make you feel better
>No, 'tis the ray on a nose not a bone
>
>Remember, one flag nation embraces
>000 flagellation, my
>sty-mule

And introduces his work to Sade who languishes in the
Bastille

writing in his cell: let no barrier restrain you: exercise at
will your right to attack or take liberties with any and all of
history's small tales, when our own pleasure is at issue.

ROUSSEAU ENTERS, INTRODUCING HIMSELF TO SADE AS RAVEN, A decent soul protected by the malevolence around it: for what sort of pleasure could one derive from seeing herds of men degraded by poverty crowding together suffocating and brutally crushing the other in the greedy struggle for a few hunks of gingerbread which have been trampled underfoot and covered in mud?

Sade will answer Rousseau's question at length later. In the meantime, this drama is interrupted by a

Dialogue Between Writing of Sade and Rousseau [2]

Writing of Rousseau: I have resolved on an enterprise which has no precedent and which, once complete, will have no imitator. So when I said that one should not talk to children about religion if one hopes that one day they will have some, I was basing my conviction on my observation—for I knew my experience did not apply to others. Let us suppose that a government is in the hands of a single individual.

Writing of Marquis de Sade: 'Tis sweet to carry out what one has fancied.

Writing of Rousseau: We see that private will cannot represent the general will, so too the general will changes its nature if it seeks to deal with an individual case: it cannot as a general will give a ruling concerning any one man or any one fact.

Writing of Marquis de Sade: Have we ever felt a single natural impulse advising us to prefer others to ourselves and is each one of us not alone, and for himself in the world?

Writing of Rousseau: This is just how a French tutor teaches his children to shine for a brief moment in childhood and then grow up into a nonentity.

Writing of Marquis de Sade: Why to be sure, and it's the ass. Are you content with your student?

Writing of Rousseau: If the inhabitant of the former consumes four and those of the latter nine, the surplus of the one will be one-fifth and of the other one-tenth.

Writing of Marquis de Sade: But your anus contracts . . . I see it.

Justine enters addressing Rousseau: Can a person who isolates himself do battle with the whole world?[3]

Conversations between France and Not–France

(Stage directions; in order to tame the body of the narrative Sade invents the narrative machine): [4]

SCENE 1: The opening [5] and enclosure [6] of great works

KITTEN: (Picks up the phone and dials.) I have just opened the windows and the dust has floated right away. Are you there Bravo? We're having Piss la Bouche with Pirouette and Hounds-lick soup for supper—at 2:30, if you can come. And please, bring something difficult.

RABBIT (a.k.a. Bravo): Who's attending?

KITTEN: The daughter's nephew's spouse, age 10, the Grandfather's son's son, age 95, Snake Man who has never married and should have nothing good to give up except that you have never met his two-by-four with which he clobbers young and old alike: he's a democrat. We've had to set up a barnyard in the abandoned cloisters to house his happy victims, who are no longer fit for society except the most flabby-holed lawyers, who pose themselves on the round rims of juleps in a strained diving posture. You know, those lawyers have set themselves up as the future educators of all the citizens. Oh, but I have forgotten the aunt of the grandfathers' mother's third daughter, who's exquisite in other ways, and she will be bringing her neighbor's children with her, as she is full of lovely excuses and a trusted soul. Now how many have I enumerated, let me go back over to make sure I haven't left any out, and you of course Bravo, one age 10, one age 95, Snake Man, we're up to three plus you and me, that makes five and the exquisite aunt I referred to that makes six and her neighbors' children are twelve or thirteen I believe so add that to, what did I say, six and you've got eighteen, nineteen, or twenty, more or less. There you have it, I will say nothing of what I plan for the day's entertainment or it will deflate your enthusiasm, but I do ask you to save a little bit of your erudition for me, so I don't have to spend all my time conniving to find a prominent position for my ass in front of your fucker.

RABBIT: We are surrounded by avalanches here. I'll have to take the military with me in order to get there at all. We'll have to pass through the Reign of Virtue: I'm not sure I'm not so sure I can risk the only feces covered militia in Not-France to a every-body-gets-what-they-want party. It's possible to pass through the Reign of Virtue with ease if we travel at night which will put us at your place around 3 a.m. But do you mind having your airy, post-revolutionary homestead surrounded by turd-infested scum?

KITTEN: Can they wash?

RABBIT: Vomits into the phone and faints.

KITTEN: Today everything must be prepared to perfection.

Kitten faxes a letter to Sardine, who she suspects is sequestered in the Chateau of Rabbit at Silling, in the only place on earth where people whose assholes compare to his reside. These people have made their appearances wearing fat and comprehensive masks in earlier literary accounts, but Sardine is new. Yet, travel books have already been written about the places to visit inside his busy orifice: the canals that have baffled even the experts of New Guinea, the volcanoes which spew over entire civilizations, and of course the industrial cacophony amusement park, just outside the PCB executive hotel, the largest conference hotel in that part of the cosmos. Once when Sardine fainted into a group of soft and unwholesome pederasts, a crowd of utopian visions floated into the sky. He had at last rid himself of The Black Empire, the Red Brigade and the Feminist Utopia, a civilization of women who orgasm whenever they want by just thinking generous thoughts about the erotic energies of another woman. After that triumphant ejection, he was unable to zip up his pants for four days until his ass had been fitted by every prick in the Silling army.

There is a lot more to tell about Sardine, especially his adventures with lawyer's children, and a theater he had constructed just for them. But it is getting late. Needless to say, Kitten is in awe of this monster even though she fantasizes his objectives as being too narrow.

Fax to Sardine from Kitten:

My wounds open as I glimpse a thousand cruel possibilities depriving me of your company. Your great skill lies in appearing to malign me while all the time humoring me and thus giving my perfidy the appearance of inspiration. Awaken the sleeping Rabbit and come in good company. I will be here with the roses.

Meow

P.S. I will pay the youths I have gathered for you once an hour until your arrival, or my financial ruin.

Rousseau enters confessing:

A shepherd born
Who faithfully swore
Nothing to fear
But never is a rose without a thorn[7]

SCENE 2: Absence of Metaphor
Number 26: Recount

Kitty put her perfect book on the shelf before picking up the phone. Rabbit was placing his perfect book on the shelf in Silling when the phone rang. The differences between Kitty and Rabbit are in the smallest details of behavior. Before Rabbit put the perfect book on the shelf he had accounted for every page of the book, answered its demands to his satisfaction, and guaranteed its perfection. As Kitty put the perfect and same book on her shelf, the Reign of Virtue came to an end.

EUGENIE: But if an action hurts a lot of people and we only like it a little bit, isn't it really pathetic to do it?

DOLMANCE: Not at all because there is no comparison between what the other experiences and what we feel. We prefer the tiniest pleasurable tickle to thoughts of others' suffering. But what's even more amazing, paradoxically, is that we enjoy others' suffering. Who would dare dispute that the suffering of others amuses us and that the absence of others' misery is a deprivation we would not wish to do without?

White End Dream

Mr. and Mrs. Falsechild were almost billionaires living in Paris.[8] Their conjugal union fructified in a daughter, the goddess of youth. On her thirteenth birthday, she made a carpet out of orange peels from the grove of their estate in the south. Mr. Falsechild had served under the Roi of Paris as the only military officer whose assets exceeded the militaries. The Roi, who was a mere shadow of former kings, being an elected official with a negligible term of office that no one kept track of and who therefore remained Roi until someone remembered to run against him, enjoyed the company of Mr. Falsechild above all others and therefore fired him in order to dine more frequently at the Falsechild's principal abode without calling attention to the affiliation. The Roi, when dropping in on Mr. Falsechild, often found him interviewing and firing tutors or polishing up his daughter to suit his tastes. The daughter sat silently behind a pale screen while the two friends dined and the Roi fancied the daughter enjoyed watching them eat. The girl's mother was almost as old as her husband and a little shrewder but she avoided berating her husband for trying to mold the tiny world of his pleasures into his own image in order to call as little attention to herself as possible. At some point, she decided she had a secret bond with the Roi, who she thought was pretending to only notice her daughter, but she never gave her husband any reason to think about her and managed her secret passion as well as she managed the household affairs behind her husband's back. Thus they lived harmoniously.

One night Miss Falsechild dreamed[9] that her false-self changed into a ferocious animal. Unrecognizable dignitaries in striated suits of mauve and green plunged her into a pool of blood floating above what appeared to be crushed cadavers. She could only make out their tails and wide-open faces looking up at her noncommittally. She cried for help from her fiancé but he didn't hear her. Her beloved cousin appeared but pulled back, disappearing into a softly lit chamber of scholarly materials. The dream left her bedridden for two days.

Finally, a party given by her mother in honor of her betrothel brought her out of bed. While seduced by the goodwill of ordinary courtship, she reserved for herself a fondness for the strange dream, which altered the world of appearances, making it more splendidly weightless for having presented to her in sleep its fouler face. This world of parties, patrimony, and play were lovely decoys for the world of death, disease, dissuatude, decay, destruction, degeneration whose synonymous distractions comforted her as she offered her hand, tilted her glass, and nodded assent in the glow of grand preparations.

When all the preparations had finally been completed, Miss Falsechild's fiancé surprised her with an urgent plea. She received the note in the morning while sitting behind the screen through which she watched the Roi and her father eating. It said:

> A furious man, whom I do not know, came to me during supper on behalf of Mr. and Mrs. Falsechild and their adoring daughter, the love of his life, whom he said returned his affections completely. He slugged me in the head, twice, the ears, the same, until I turned on him. A four-hour battle ensued. His face now rests ensnared at the bottom of a blood bath. I am giving you twenty-four hours to explain this and renew your affections.

Suppressed names and their propositions

Those from Whom it holds
to Madame: I
snap. Dolmance: all
has been said
the irresistible desire between twistings
authorized by your very own spouse

1. Jean-Jacques Rousseau, *Confessions,* and Marquis de Sade, *Philosophy in the Bedroom.*

2. The dialogue is created from Jean-Jacques Rousseau's *The Social Contract* and Marquis de Sade's *Philosophy in the Bedroom,* which is drawn from and exploited in other parts of the text.

3. *Justine* by Marquis de Sade.

4. From *Literary Fortifications: Rousseau, Laclos, Sade* by Joan DeJean.

5. Opening: 1795, at the time of the Directory.

6. Enclosure: 1785, in the Bastille.

7. A song of Rousseau's nanny from *The Confessions* by Jean-Jacques Rousseau.

8. The story that follows is an adaptation of *Faxelange, ou le tort de l'ambition* by Marquis de Sade.

9. Dreamed: Everything that was material, was potential, was present had been altered by the concept of white and this is why: dreams are secret movements that can not be assigned a "true place." Somewhere outside the pool of blood was a schoolroom full of ordinary children. For dreams mock human dishonesty and use up time. The overcast classroom, the indeterminent faces, the square floor tiling, wood desks, sharpened pencils, smells of lead dust filings, the diagonal light jetting across the floor with the dust particles mixing round, the door left slightly ajar to let the swath of light enter but not too ajar so as to function also as a barrier to outdoor noises, other children, and potential escapees. It is never wrong to listen to what dreams have to offer us, as in this case of which I will continue to speak: the teacher is beautiful. No one can understand why such a beautiful teacher teaches in such an ordinary setting in spite of the ordinariness of her teaching. She has told us it is wrong to go against what we have learned of philosophy to use dreams superstitiously as predictions of events that have not yet come to pass. In waiting day after day for the results, turning these nonevents into the sole object of our devotion what are we trying to prove? She continues her lesson by explaining the phenomenon of color, ending in white, because, she says, "White is the end." Miss Falsechild, with the streak of gray, nearly white hair that illuminates the abundance of shining dark maelstrom around it, objects to this idea of white and after class makes her objections. "The dream is the result of an event that has already taken place. White is not the end.

The spirit of a dream is to provide us with an opening, where a new face surfaces on an already familiar event. You can follow the movement of a painting through the action of whiteness, in either abstract or representational works." That was her argument.

Dreams are never madness.

"I will bring you an example," she told her teacher, but she wondered if her teacher knew what she meant by abstraction. She began the campaign for her argument by going through books with reproductions of Malevich and realized that her point about white had been insignificant; yet, she did note that in the artist Amy Attractovich's collage, which now faced her as she sat at her dresser, white had been used by the renaissance artist whose work the collagist had coopted in a manner that created a feeling of vibrating yet peaceful depth charges.

Without dreams we are ignorant of our father's actions and are brought up in the greatest absurdity.

Amy Attractovitch had painted a few white swaths on one side of the collage as part of the alteration of the original, forcing some images of women back into a dream of history, leaving the new white, blunted paint as a presence, unknowable but to be contended with as if an interruption in a dream.

Dreams are nature, which we force ourselves on analytically. In this way, we resemble foolish alchemists wasting their energies on the production of gold flecks.

My god, thinks our contemporary American Miss Falsechild, is this what the teacher means by "White is the end?" It can't be. There is and must be an urgent vibrating motion that illuminates the past through present actions. White is the instigator of power as moving force. There are so many cases of white, for instance, the white of Jasper Johns. Why didn't I think of Jasper Johns in class? But the thought of him turned gray before it had completed itself as white. Once she fully recollected the white that she was trying to restore to its true place, she realized that she was thinking about Ad Rhenhardt Well, that is a relief. He's a better example. White is not the end. Or is it? The dreams cut us down in our pursuit of them.

As she searched the art books, her teacher's words clung to the other side of every argument. I am agitated, and so I am the white of my own representation, but the teacher is referring to a white in her symbolic order and if I try to prove my point, whenever I try to prove this point, her argument will represent itself as the possibility of symbolic meaning. Now white appears to me as it does to her, as the end, and what had at one time appeared as a dynamic force bursting out of possibility (white), looks like the moment of abandonment, before which colors disappear. And our inability to understand dreams destroys us. Our ill-conceived efforts are also part of our destruction. As in a vortex, white is taking the color back.

We are cut down by our own efforts, but our destruction is not everything, because each thing or event in nature is entirely particular to itself, and in making their condition separate, nature creates consequences in dreams that we can never divine.

THAT CANNOT BE TAKEN AWAY FROM IT

WHO HAS NOT BEEN SLEEPING ON AN INSPIRED DAY? THE MIND OF the day sleeps us. Watching us. A fascinated consciousness. That thing that cannot be taken away from it. There are no bad feelings and no spectacle.[1] Or the day spits at a spectacle it finds at work transferring illusion to illusion to conceal the lack of ocean it needs to make the illusion at night thrive when the day has left us with its head striking, falling blankly into a name, as if a name were a head striking a mug, a filial alphabet, an enumerated pause.

"One, nine, and eleven are femaling me" said a voice at a distance.

In Mexico there are many more flowering trees. Some violet. Painted sand swirls up from the painted desert and drives into the car. Hence, the birth of an idea or a sea. An ocean of flowering trees.

How is it to be phrased? Are we going to phrase it? As if a pantry had opened on its own, revealing the source of the strange family's well-being, the family is going to be phrased by us. The automaton provides endless variations on this pep talk while we methodically eat through our cage. The automaton feels an excruciating physical discomfort because the direction of its energy is unknown to itself. This causes the seated parts to wish to stand and the standing parts to wish to sit.

In the meantime, the strange family sleeps. Its posture, and all its variations (the sleeping standing, the seated sleeping, the waking slept and sleeping, the dreaming waking finishing touches the touching sleeping, and all the endless family ties of seated waking in one's sleep) is as accurate as conventional uses of punctuation. And in all the darting of these postures, ambitions out in all directions, they share a common source in the Universe that has never been seen. I have been told that it will disappear if you call it by its name. An euphoric scent reminds the family of itself.

It is a tradition that introducing ambition into a work of art foreshadows future moral complications. One is going to wake and dream and sleep and one is going to wake and sleep and dream. A man is talking on the phone non-stop through all of this. The radio is glowing about his presence. It is going on and on about it. It is the mouthpiece for the man, and although he does not lack ambition, he is not the subject of this discussion.

Photographs represent the subject of a longed-for life. One can also think of sexuality as clinical. Behavior is an essence we can't help. "When she rose to her own defense she was sought after by many parties." In the center of one of these parties is blind ambition waiting to get her. She had been in bed when her lover told her to stop napping, so she woke and went to work, but her lover was not there at all. He was speaking to someone else. And so she went to the party by herself. The sand in the desert rose in the painted air.

You do not now need your ambitions, family. It is pulled by magnets an inert door. They all knock up against the door and stick there until it opens. This is the door to the party. Inside, everyone is loosely defined. "I feel strange," says the daughter waking on the sleeping brother's shoulder. Psychologically slick peepholes spring into existence.

A rocklike character from the South Seas arrives. A quantitative person with large inhalations. There are causal relations one must resist drawing with respect to him. It takes "infinite patience" or industrious spirits to maintain things as they are, not what they appear to illuminate around them.

And so this is Robert Desnos.[2]
The room is closed and empty, quite empty.
It is light and there is too much sun.
But not here, look at these people.
There are . . .
Many of us . . .
Robert, did you say?
Who would not have come had we known.
It's hard to get out of here.
Yah, Desnos, you know.
Desnos.

Say the people in the party.

"I can almost do this in my sleep," said the rocklike character taking a deep breath. The door in the palm of his hand opened briefly and closed. It went too fast to see much of anything, but the strange father was left with the impression of acres of land.

"Do you like who you are?" asked the baby looking directly at the rocklike character. The baby was chewing on a swollen cactus. The baby was in the desert the father had seen through the door. Of course, what she was eating could double as a weapon. "It's very hard," said the baby, "to figure all of this out."

Anywhere is the subject of the baby's quandary. When she is older, a scent from a tree she has never seen will transport her. This, while she is answering some rudimentary question: "No, that is not mine." She also refuses some slang, which is given to her lightly. And she is away, this away being a set. Her work is complete. Quandary, variation, quandary, variation, pause. The set is complete. She is transported to an inert door. Behind the door, a family. She is traveling through a vast desert. The family holds her kite. Abstraction holds her up. And no one is there in this funny figure. Set. In air.

What is your name?

It's going to be Fred. It's going to be Louise. No matter what, it's a big success. This corruption lies flat in deep water. Who are we to pull it out? Whoever you may be, the broad plain awaits you. The desert birds are poised. The weeds pose. Someone is hoping it will be himself/herself Himself/herself slept by the day, is part of a dream that shoulders the limits of sleep as it works its way across water.

Himself/herself prods us with questions. Who are we to answer? Himself/herself eases into a boat. The story of the boat: these little birds are sitting there. The mother counts them all. The hand of any hand. The door of any door. Stops. And so at a party, there are no mothers and daughters, there are no sons. The fathers eat in an obscure room and people laugh at them for having to be there where they will not make themselves welcome by virtue of their insatiable identities. Fathers, stop talking to yourselves. You act like lunatics. That is what the childless, parentless population cries as they drunkenly pass the open door.

Night turns its back on the boat which made a bad bargain in exchange for sleep the trader had bought but couldn't use. Now it is sunning, assuming nothing. "I must find a way out of storage," said the boat and came to us for advice. It offered us an account of the first years of life: in the building was a building. Once upon a time, the building was built. Though the building was settled, it became more remote. But we have no building we said to the boat.

The boat in the shallow lagoon sat heavy on our thoughts as we froze in the wilderness for want of a place to live, for we had been thrust from our houses at an early age as a tribute to our ability to survive. We were then carried by the air and set here. When we saw himself/herself we strained to recall the party, where we had been introduced. Some kind of overlap had volunteered our socially respectable names, in that we had names. One per person.

1. A staged simulation of spectacular video techniques: stage lighting and sets interact in such a way as to produce the electronic glow from the TV set: figures are structured into the geometrical pattern projected on screens in the set, contributing an archaic symmetry (that of the human body) to the modern. The spectacle uses the human body to adorn itself at the same time the actor's beautiful singing adorns the spectacle. Beauty has been created from any angle, and the horror of the universe would be entirely left out if it were not for the fact that any illusion can lead the mind into its own endless realm of illusions. Now inside the potential of one's fears, one looks into the staged illusion and is struck (or captured) by awe in spite of the empty vagaries of techniques. Hence, a depth is created in oneself which seems to exist inherently in what is on stage. This is the secret of dramatic arts.

2. The first line is from "The Airtight Room," a poem by Robert Desnos, translated by Mary Ann Caws.

THE ROCK

THE ROCK TURNS ON ITS HIND LEGS AND PLEADS INNOCENCE. IT filches a panoply of events. It lurches into mother's room and comes out shocked. That is the condition of the rock.

A rock blinks at a timetable.

The rock walks to the end of the plank.

The rock makes a splash.

It is the last we have heard of the rock.

The rock is well, it is better. It has recovered. It has come back to life. It has come back to haunt us. It is eating away at our house. It is taking our fortune with it. It is going down again. It is a destructive rock. This is the last time we will let it in the door.

It nuzzles against our fence and befriends the dog.

It helps old people cross the street. Some of our neighbors feel sorry for the rock. It hangs its head outside the laundromat and gives away quarters if you're out. You don't have to ask it to guard your clothes. It also stands guard in the night and fawns over your front axle and tires.

For the feel of rubber, it will grow old before its time and crumble into the gutter. Someday a weed will grow, where there once was rock. It will not care for other's safety, only its own. I will let the weeds grow to my door. I will let them take over. I will be safe inside. I will look out the window, sigh, grow old and happy. I will live all the rest of my life in great relief. For I have touched the rock and now it's gone. I have struck the rock with my nasty tongue. I have dislodged the rock with my uncaring gaze. I'm the devil. I'm the rock.

I shred the innocence off the rock and filch its panoply of events. The boulevard is full of empty duds! This is the road to behavior. This is the street of sighs. I will take my weeds with me and march among military songs, who rock the civilized word to sleep at the same time they polish monuments and clutter up the empty duds. Heave to for shiny buildings! I touch this clever clutter of sleep and it is the wrong move. Some nighttime kiss I hang over the railing for. I am not in my own country but someone else's nest. I can't simply walk into that story.

The next move must be negotiated. I touch the intellect and it feels cold and nasty. I have been taped to a device.

History is nowhere.

That is not what I think. It's what's been already thought. He feels he is a woman in search of a man.

Hence, an *intense interest in railways.*

I don't see myself in the mirror. I don't look in it now, but toward the intense interest. Manifested within an excruciating hunger, it feeds upon the restaurant until collapsing from exhaustion. Someone must recover the body. She hasn't died, nor does she seem to be dead, yet there is a body, a shape. Who should not be here unless dressed. The stranger dislodges the shape from the hearth of the cocktail lounge.

The street is never empty.

Anything she hears while in his arms must be relevant. This is no doubt the only justifiable basis for what in other respects is the questionable practice of ascribing nervous disorders to intellectual "overwork." The tomb was a fraud.

When they arrived at the arena, the place was seething with lust for cruelty. She fell and fell more pitifully than the man whose fall had drawn that roar of excitement from the crowd. The din had pierced her ears and forced her to open her eyes.

Afterward, it was snowing and she was asleep in the cart. She wanted to wake up. The stranger touched her as if she'd not been dressed. But she could feel her coat around her. Puzzled by this sensation, she knelt at the foot of some high steps. They were moving downward. A little ways away, among the snow and exposed rubble, people were eating the ground. Hunger and the fear that someone would see through her cape caused her to cringe when a pebble rolled toward her. With her gaze, she followed the trace of its path. It was a theoretical path. It was the end in itself. Deletion equals it.

Anything named slips out of the mind. The sexual instinct becomes altruistic. I am going to fleece you. When she touched a stair, it sank like dough. She wept with exceeding weeping and her father wept too to see her in a cape which reminded him of his separation from his mother. The eunuch pitied him and they ate together until satisfied.

Dimly the girl recognized that this event excluded her regardless of the attention it attracted from bystanders who by now are wandering in search of their own daughters, or mothers, to weep over. She also guesses rightly that if it were not for a present obsession of her own, she would be enraged by this attention a eunuch and her helpless father could command. Their tears and pity created their tears and pity in others. In fact, the force of her repulsion had torn her from the domesticated universe.

The stairs descended within their phony passage of time. The walls of the enclosure inspired feelings of omnipotence.

With clubs of oak she attacked the image. Someone touched her on the back as if she were undressed. She told the cop to get lost and continued to pillage the monument. There was no entree except the mutuality she had denied.

Now the sky moves toward subterranean jargon.

But who were those good people?

It was night again and the dream rattled down the boulevard. Her body was heavy rolling from side to side in the cart. This sensation was more satisfying than all the nets in Detroit. The driver sang and sang, badly. His voice grated at her heart. And yet the song protected her weakened powers with the replaceability of its parts. This is what happened, but it could have been something else.

Something else was there. This unknown threat walked back and forth in front of a swamp. It stopped and loosened its tie. It could not shake free of its own weight. The repulsive monument fell into a stupor.

There is a potential cartoon within any manifestation of destruction. She slapped the tips of the prematurely chuckling trees. Their branches splintered and fell into perfect piles of firewood.

Whatever the child animates is lost to us.

The list of governmental grievances against the citizenry was too detailed to exhibit in public. So instead, a man in a tuxedo and a woman in a blue dress were employed to walk down the street on a bright day. Then they eat and drink and kiss and clip necks and in this way abide till evening when she gives him money because she finds his weaving nice and good.

He bows deeply and sleeps among the ruins. Waking in the moonlight, he sees a woman sliding underground. And thus he is reminded of what he is.

Something moves.

The rock turns on its hind legs to plead innocence but its captors are a mile away. What it sees is a woman escaping underground. Thinking, it can't move, and moving it can't think. How could that woman so easily sink? It tries to change its behavior and affirm family life. Its mother is in no mood to talk and it runs away shocked.

The red and filthy captors mount their cattle and belch.

The red and filthy captors dig deep into their pockets. The mayor comes by to take what they've dug up. We are thus warned to loosen the bond that exists in our thoughts between instinct and object.

Like trains heralding words, the new day brightens

the repulsive monument waking from its stupor to witness this clamor among the socially compromised. The lake sinks in passing and the city blocks nestle in their captions. The dark brick on the floor of a painted dragon removes some wings. Walls snatch them up in an absorptive passion. So too the lessons are undone. The length of waiting triples. Flies maneuver to occupy the treeless pate. Sand punishes the hose. And the slowness of the rows bakes within a can of beans. Lies also go unpunished. The communal spirit does not comprehend anything measured with lines. There is a welling of people at low tide.

Rocks, blow to the head of the class!

Now the lake is empty when we want it to be fun.

The singing children grew up in front of the speed-way and a rock reared up in its repressed anger, for it had lately been beaten down by a lute *en route* to Brussels. The singing children grew wary in face of the betrothed whose instincts ran the show while hollowing out the ground of our speechless times.

THE MALE

WOULD YOU PREFER THE EXAMPLES? THE PANCAKES? OR THE WORDS?

Oh, I have been used as an example so many times, said the Male. I think I . . . Do I? Do I think? said the Male.

Pancakes are good, I reminded him.

If, said the Male, I say anything, I reveal something of myself: my stupidity, or arrogance, or inability to make selections. I can't speak . . .

If you could only make a choice, I could say, for example, well the Male prefers pancakes and that must mean something. Words pain the Male, I could say. And then I would attempt to apply that information as an example. Everybody would be able to make sense out of the expression *the male's pancakes*. When in the galleries, I could point to the portrait of an ancestor and say "the male's pan-cakes," and everyone would laugh from the pleasure that words and things can so transform each other they make the most sense when used in tandem.

I have always liked the word *tandem,* said the Male, seemingly inspired or abstracted by a distant shadow creeping slowly over his brow.

You are not concentrating!

Con-cen-tra-ting? said the Male. The pressure to concentrate is very heavy, I imagine.

You imagine? I asked.

I can't quite make it out, so I would say I do imagine . . .

The Male stood next to a rock in a large bed of rocks at the top of the near-bald hill. Some sheep ran up the hill, pulled at turf, and descended to richer pastures.

We climbed side by side to an old fort where the Welsh had defended themselves from the Vikings. The wind was so strong, I had to climb on my hands and knees because I was pregnant. I would rest against a mound on the hillside and the Male would disappear in a trough in the hill. I would look down to an empty swimming pool behind a farmhouse. The pool had probably been out of use since the renovation of the Roman canals where boatloads of people now traveled along a steamy strip of water above the town, unseen by the people in the town below. One person from the town stuck out in my reflections, a woman with pruning shears standing in a driveway arguing with a man whose car she had had towed.

A lot more heavy breathing on the part of jealous neighbors and the Male asked me, is a poet a poet all the time? I don't like riddles and didn't want to answer the question. The Male, however was desperately serious, singing out the following verse:

> These loud birds
> Flying above the cathedral
> Counter the politeness
> That keeps me anonymous
>
> Noise makes drama
> Out of ruins
> The trees develop in the ruins
> An authoritative base for birds

Was this the poetry of prose? The Male by nature prosaic, moving from one place to the next in an unrhapsodic way, thinking hard perhaps but communicating little, allowing his motions to speak for him, so that he was followed by a trail of his own making? Would others follow this trail, each having their own experience of it, each wondering what it was like for anyone else to have been there? (For instance, what was it like for Orphan Annie? The cranky-looking filling station out the window? The hoses on the pumps having lost their resilience? The attendant limp as grease? The comic strip reader in a sunlit, airy place?) Life is like a book, any book, even technical manuals.

On the other hand, there is the body, a form, and who knows what goes on in the Male's mind? The Male would exhibit a deep, ponderous blank. And yet, *I* do not have a verse in any of my thoughts. Is a landowner a landowner *all* the time? The landowner would either say "yes" or "no, I'm just a person."

I am just a person, I said to the Male, but you are not just a male. I don't know why I chose to present myself in this way to the creature.

What can you tell me about the *faux-naïf*? asked the Male.

There is something in your question that reminds me of masturbating while reading Wordsworth. The reader effaces the merits of the poet's journey at the same time as she follows it with enthusiasm. A great inarticulateness has overcome her as she encounters the high rhetoric.

We were standing against the crumbling wall of the fort as I spoke. The wind was taking my words away from me. The Male was still watching the sheep race back to richer pastures long after they had reached that destination. It is possible to become very fond of a trace, a story that is always the same.

Epilogue

Rituals are like ducks in pink water, says the Male. Like everything else he says, this is from out of the blue. In the background Baudelaire imitates an orator: If I am not decorated for having done my duty, I will cease to do it . . . Words come to the Male. They are not willed into being. There is a sinking feeling at the end of any utterance. The last word may by accident use up the potential of all the others. Then the pitch downward will be into the eternity of the Male mind, his endless spontaneity and lack of preference. When I drink pink water out of the bowl shaped from his head, he looks at my throat. Bolus, says the Male. This seems to cover up some kind of disparity. The desire to be touched is overwhelming. But whose desire is it? This relates to our initial conversation, where one word could be taken to the land of many.

MY STORY

SPEAKING IN A STATE OF FIDELITY TO THE SUBJECT, LIVING FLESH though it may be, is similar to assuming one has acquired the song of birth through the ritual repeating of the names and gestures of newborn infants. This makes me want to cry. But I can't lie: no way am I going to disguise myself in the habit of that body, the one that isn't mine.

My story will never turn out because of the mass surrounding its small and devious posturings. Assuming the tone of reverence, an author describes a woman climbing a hill.

This is a braggart's tale. It starts in the endless heart-lands of a dull plain when looked at from the point of view of a small animal. Perhaps a snail travels along the borders ceaselessly making the visible world the token of some larger obliteration.

I was born but do not understand that phenomenon any better than whatever creature may never think about it. I, however, am not perplexed. Incognito striplings suspend the rapidly changing paths of life. Their job is to curtail the disappearance of whatever has failed to be held up for observation, to keep potential beasts from jumping into deep and invisible water before they have been judiciously examined by Expertise, that changeling hanging supine over the town of Nemole, the farthest point from the border. In the interest of the flesh, the striplings dine out every so often, showing their teeth, their raunchy ways, and heckling anyone who offers to see them by rippling the fur on their necks.

Childhood doesn't exist. Infancy is out of the question. I mastered the things I have forgotten. Aggrieved, I lose jokes to the stepping-stone mentality employed by one's associates and so on. The striplings kept to their course and I to mine. I couldn't console them. They couldn't show me my face.

PORTRAITS

ONE WANTS TO EAT CERTAIN WORDS, BECAUSE THEY ARE PERFECT
and embarrassments as well. "Lacking" is an example.
Another is "somnambulistic": DeQuincy, the hallucinator as
the bride of a Victorian lady who has been shattered by hal-
lucinations that in turn strictly hold her severity in place.
DeQuincy the female male wears a magnificent ring passed
down through centuries by the Victorian lady's family, all of
whom were either pirates or paupers. He is in "drag" wearing the great pirates' formal clothing, but underneath is the
hard-breasted and tough-wombed body of the pauper. His
androgynous complexity draws rings of discourse around
the Victorian female's fainting Cartesian viewpoint.

The

Inside the box of words is where the woman appears. It is not possible to be that female man. Or TO BE anything that follows in the footpath of his waking dream. Dream is another of those perfect and perfectly embarrassing words, pivoting on a misery styled to something greater. In the manner of a young woman in a novel coming out as if she'd always been out there, the dream is a resounding grand ballroom of interpretation. It is ceremonial. Thus, on the long march down the clown's (afraid of its gender) sleeve on the way to the sneak harvest, the women in this cacophonous utopia (as deep as a dimple, as long as an arm, and as wide as labia or lips) interpret themselves as portraits.

Therefore, the lady in white is nowhere. A slick density of tongue pronounces an empty place. The lungs go in and out but remain pictorially flat. The gullet is as airy as starvation. Inside the lady in white, the senses record only dark and light. The veins are filled with heavenly water, in which nothing can grow. This liquid is pumped to the heart, which occurs in her as a fetish regulating the pure liquid river of her life and the dark and light finessings of her senses. Pedantic and iconoclastic, her stomach holds an untouched schoolroom, one that children will never enter. Never will a child get away with murder or sit in the teacher's desk rummaging through the teacher's drawers in secret! There's no door to this haven of pedagogy, only an inside view hooked up to whorls of pearlescent intestines nestled between marble and granite organs: the liver, kidneys, pancreas ecstatically illuminated by the current of purest liquid flowing among the veins, all witnesses and watchdogs in a

Cleopatrean bath of denatured aura, which circles her soft-
est of wombs composed of feathers found only on the bellies
of white egrets.

In the bend of the arm of the Amazon is a cave.
Inside this cave is a civilization of the ghosts of the ghosts of
women. Here comes one now. "I am the ghost of the ghost
of Clytemnestra, the husband murderer. I live in California
in a neoconservative chapel constructed out of Somalian
handicrafts. When the first ghost of Clytemnestra died in a
harangue and passed through the Desert Storm to a place
freshly titled The Greater Good, I rose from the two-thou-
sand-year-old corpse without a sense of time. I did not know
how to function in a world with time, so I slipped into the
first cave I could find: this one, whose entrance can be found
inside the bend of the arm of the Amazon, Mona. She who
hunts, makes love, makes war, eats, sleeps but little else.
Inside, we do all the talking. It is a great comfort to her that
she can share her happiness with us; although, if she could
see it, I do believe she would find our Californian civilization
disturbing. It is more work than one can possibly imagine,
this civilization, our lab. Mona probably doesn't even know
the meaning of the word laboratory! My job is to simulate
the fears of women-haters. My Job? Clytemnestra, whose
hatred was as complete as divine projection re-creates herself as I work with this as a job title: Simulator of the Fears of
Women-Haters. I bet you'd like to know what she would say
if she could speak.

The sky has all the moods of the day: today, tomor-
row and yesterday. Sometimes the moods are called hope,
obscurity and agony. The sky woman, sometimes known as
the Keeper of the Spool Babies, although this is really a mis-

nomer for reasons to be narrated later, lives inside the moods of the day in a voluptuous protoplasmic completeness unimaginable to all but certain birds of prey. What does she bring to this comic packet? The whispering of hope, the lectures of obscurity, and *tête-à-têtes* wander in and out of her folds of luscious flesh. Once a whisper fell into a potato field surrounded by deltas and suspension bridges and rubbed itself out digging for a root in a pungent ripple. So many words have been lost in her flesh that the mood of loss follows her wherever she goes.

The woman in white's visceral knowledge must be somewhere. The Amazon's detached utopian impulses to harbor the ghosts of ghosts and her concomitant commitment to remaining ignorant of their experiments must manifest itself in a more pragmatic manner somewhere. The sky woman's rushing plumpness must be touchable from somewhere. No woman is an island.

Yet, the she devil, Interpretation, sets herself in a fixed position. Dependent entirely on external circumstances and yet entirely unpredictable in her treatment of them, she of the blunted lips, looks on as two repair people pass in a white truck with the word SOLVENTS inscribed on it in black letters. "Did you see that person sitting on a crossbeam?" asks the team. Interpretation remains silent. Next a child eating a Mr. Goodbar bicycles by with candy in one hand, steering the bike with the other. Interpretation again explains nothing. A cop on a motorcycle stops in front of her but does not look in her direction. I wonder why not she thinks. But she does not speak. The Japanese author Tanizaki walks past her perch at the construction site as well. He recognizes her on her unorthodox perch. "You," he says, "enjoy being noticed." "And you," she parrots, "enjoy being noticed." "Yes," he says, "there is something on which we agree." "Yes, there is something on which we agree," she says. He says, "I will return here later." "I will return here later," she says also. An ocean breeze catches the lip of her sleeve as Tanazaki disappears in the distance. Interpretation remains in her fixed position seated on the cross-beam in a construction site. Dust flies around her as the breeze picks up. She curves her back and lowers her square forehead. Her low brows push her blunted lips out in a semi-pout. There is something wrong in the Realm of Interpretation. Interpretation! Oh, Interpretation. What will happen to you when the crane and shovel arrive with the crew? Where will you go? What will you do?

Mrabet, Mohammed. THE BOY WHO SET THE FIRE
Mrabet, Mohammed. THE LEMON
Mrabet, Mohammed. LOVE WITH A FEW HAIRS
Mrabet, Mohammed. M'HASHISH
Murguía, A. & B. Paschke, eds. VOLCAN: Poems from Central America
Murillo, Rosario. ANGEL IN THE DELUGE
Parenti, Michael. AGAINST EMPIRE
Pasolini, Pier Paolo. ROMAN POEMS
Pessoa, Fernando. ALWAYS ASTONISHED
Peters, Nancy J., ed. WAR AFTER WAR (City Lights Review #5)
Poe, Edgar Allan. THE UNKNOWN POE
Porta, Antonio. KISSES FROM ANOTHER DREAM
Prévert, Jacques. PAROLES
Purdy, James. THE CANDLES OF YOUR EYES
Purdy, James. GARMENTS THE LIVING WEAR
Purdy, James. IN A SHALLOW GRAVE
Purdy, James. OUT WITH THE STARS
Rachlin, Nahid. THE HEART'S DESIRE
Rachlin, Nahid. MARRIED TO A STRANGER
Rachlin, Nahid. VEILS: SHORT STORIES
Reed, Jeremy. DELIRIUM: An Interpretation of Arthur Rimbaud
Reed, Jeremy. RED-HAIRED ANDROID
Rey Rosa, Rodrigo. THE BEGGAR'S KNIFE
Rey Rosa, Rodrigo. DUST ON HER TONGUE
Rigaud, Milo. SECRETS OF VOODOO
Ross, Dorien. RETURNING TO "A"
Ruy Sánchez, Alberto. MOGADOR
Saadawi, Nawal El. MEMOIRS OF A WOMAN DOCTOR
Sawyer-Lauçanno, Christopher, transl. THE DESTRUCTION OF THE JAGUAR
Scholder, Amy, ed. CRITICAL CONDITION: Women on the Edge of Violence
Sclauzero, Mariarosa. MARLENE
Serge, Victor. RESISTANCE
Shepard, Sam. MOTEL CHRONICLES
Shepard, Sam. FOOL FOR LOVE & THE SAD LAMENT OF PECOS BILL
Smith, Michael. IT A COME
Snyder, Gary. THE OLD WAYS
Solnit, Rebecca. SECRET EXHIBITION: Six California Artists
Sussler, Betsy, ed. BOMB: INTERVIEWS
Takahashi, Mutsuo. SLEEPING SINNING FALLING
Turyn, Anne, ed. TOP TOP STORIES
Tutuola, Amos. FEATHER WOMAN OF THE JUNGLE
Tutuola, Amos. SIMBI & THE SATYR OF THE DARK JUNGLE
Valaoritis, Nanos. MY AFTERLIFE GUARANTEED
Veltri, George. NICE BOY
Wilson, Colin. POETRY AND MYSTICISM
Wilson, Peter Lamborn. SACRED DRIFT
Wynne, John. THE OTHER WORLD
Zamora, Daisy. RIVERBED OF MEMORY

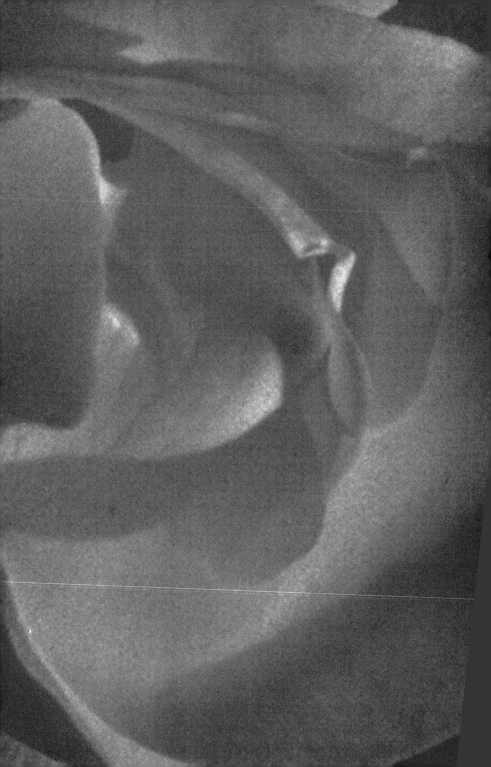